MURDER AT NUTHATCH NEST

NICOLETTE HARPFORD

PRINT ISBN-13: 979-8-9876688-0-1

Cover Design: BookCoverZone

Edition: First

Printing: Second

Published by Avenue du Gui

CONTENTS

Chapter One

GREAT AUNT LOIS

With the exception of a couple of red-breasted nuthatches perching on the crumbling stone fence of a farmer's field, the landscape is quiet. Large, papery snowflakes pattern my windshield as I turn my car to meet a decrepit looking lane hidden beside a crumbling pile of rocks. The road looks poorly paved and seldom used. It's bordered by two fields before they peter out and thick foliage takes over. I'm tempted to turn around and avoid the road all together, but the sky opens up and serves as a reminder of the impending winter storm. With a heavy push from the heavens, the wind rustles my car, and a cascade of fresh flakes covers the windows. I push my foot lightly to the pedal before I can change my mind about venturing towards the dreary lane.

The woods that edge against the road are thick with trees and plants. I recognize the remnants of black walnut droppings as the tennis ball-like fruit litters part of the forest floor that hasn't yet been covered with snow. Thick poison ivy vines lick their way up several pines grouped close together, and an old-looking Magnolia shivers as ice dangles from its limbs. Normally when I think of snow, I think about the saccharine Christmas cards my boss's wife usually sends out once a year with tiny villages covered in white glitter, not of gloomy trees huddled together for warmth.

The thought of work sends an excited buzz through me, so I take a deep breath to calm myself. I've worked for *The Binocular Feather Feature Birding Magazine*, more often referred to by its nickname "The BFF Birding Magazine," since I graduated college with my journalism degree. I wasn't a huge birder when I was hired, but I didn't let that stop me from working for a prestigious nature magazine. It took time and effort, but I can now consider myself an experienced birdwatcher.

My current writing credits are strictly limited to "The Backyard Bird Blurb," a tiny section in the magazine dedicated to hints and tips for spotting common songbirds throughout the country, but this past summer marked my fifth year at the magazine, and with enough persistence, I managed to convince Mr. Hawking, my editor, to let me write a story that has the potential to land on the cover. The article will be an in-depth look at *Nuthatch Nest*, a famous house built in the 1800s by a recluse in dedication to his wife, the daughter of a famed ornithologist. Her favorite bird happened to be the white-breasted nuthatch, hence the name.

It wasn't an easy story to land, but it happened to be one unique to me that Mr. Hawking couldn't pass on to one of the more experienced writers. The current owner of the house just happens to be my Great Aunt Lois, and she only agreed to the article on the condition that her great niece was the one to write it. I would only be fooling myself if I didn't admit to being a bit nervous though. Despite the familial relation, I don't really know Lois. According to my mother, the last time I saw Lois was when she dropped by my second birthday party about twenty-five years ago. Other than that, our only communication has been the one phone call I made in which I asked her permission to write the story. She seemed to remember me though.

My GPS announces I've arrived at my destination. Ahead, the road bends, and a blind curve is enveloped by leaves and dense wood. I haven't been to Great Aunt Lois's house before, but I'm guessing it must be behind the bend. I wonder if she has many visitors. It would be difficult to convince anyone to visit a house hidden away in the woods like this one. I put my car in park and grab the bright red coat that goes over my winter fleece. At least if I get lost while trying to find my way, I'll be easy to spot against the snowy backdrop.

Before I can get out of the car and enjoy the smattering of falling snow and give my legs a stretch, my phone buzzes. It's my parents. It's not unusual for them to call at odd hours of the day. I wonder where in the world they are at this moment. Alaska? Greece? When Meg, my youngest sister, finished college, my parents shocked everyone by announcing that they were selling our childhood home and going to live on cruise ships, in hotels, and in the guest rooms of family members and friends as they flitted around the globe. I felt stunned as I sat across from them at dinner while they smiled at their three daughters. Meg, ever the dreamer, thought it was a fantastic idea. Could she meet up with them if they took a trip to Tahiti? Kiera, my older sister, just about threw the table across the room at the news—firing off questions about Social Security and IRAs. And me? I, typical of myself, just sat there, stunned at the news.

"Hey, Mom," I say into the phone.

"Emma..." My mother's voice comes through the phone in static swoops.

"Where are you?" I ask.

"We're in Ponta Delgada!" The static dissolves away as if she's moved to a new location. "Your father and I had the most amazing hiking trip yesterday. Beautiful! And the food! Amazing! Your dad is a bit sunburned from spending too much time at the beach this morning though. That reminds me, I need to pick up some aloe vera in the hotel gift shop."

"Mom," I say before she can go into detail about the condition of my father's skin. "Is everything alright?"

"We're calling to see if you arrived at Great Aunt Lois's place."

"If my GPS is correct, then I have. It's a bit deserted though."

"Deserted? That sounds about right! Your father and I only visited her once. Of course, it was back when Uncle Albert was still alive, but I do remember the house being a bit off the beaten path. It must be lonely for Lois living there all by herself now."

"You're right about it looking lonely, and it certainly isn't centrally located either. My mood also isn't helped by the fact that I have no memories of either Great Aunt Lois or Great Uncle Albert."

"You don't have any memories of Great Uncle Albert? You must remember Uncle Albert! Remember, he was the one who always had those stories about spies and missing art that he would tell over the holidays? He had worked for some private detective agency!"

"Mom, I have absolutely no recollection of anyone that exciting being in our family. I think you're getting Great Uncle Albert mixed up with someone you met on a cruise."

"A man I met on a cruise?" My mother lets out a sigh. "I guess it's just as well. Your father does have more relatives than I can count." This wasn't an exaggeration on my mother's part. Every time I went to visit my grandparents, another long-lost relative would drop by.

There is a short pause in the conversation when a large, black bird swoops near the front of my windshield, startling me, before disappearing into the darkening woods. Without having enough time to think about feather patterns or chest color, the identification of the bird is already lost to me. Some birding expert I am.

"Mom, I better go. It's getting darker here, and I want to get to Great Aunt Lois's house before the light completely disappears."

"Before the light disappears? I didn't realize it was so late over there. It's so hard to keep track of what time it is across the globe. I love you, honey. Have a nice time with Great Aunt Lois!"

I thrust my car door open a little more aggressively than intended. The contrast between the warm car and the freezing air stuns me when I step outside, and my cheeks sting with the cold burn of the temperature. I don't bother locking my car. Anyone who tries to steal it won't get very far very fast in this weather. I let out a breath that curls, a twisty trail of shower-like steam, and head towards the bend in the road ahead.

As soon as I take a sharp turn at the bend, the texture beneath my boots changes from old pavement to stone, and the road turns into a narrow walking path. Good thing my GPS didn't direct me to drive any farther. Up ahead, a metal gate appears. It's covered in dying weeds and orange rust. Against the light snow, the rust glows like embers, beckoning me to continue on my way. The gate is small enough to hop over, but I can see that on the other side some sort of low, dense bush grows against it, so it's probably better to go through the gate if it hasn't rusted shut. The lock lifts up easily. I lean my body against the metal opening until it gives. A loud screech, the sound of the rusty metal sliding on the ground, echoes through the woods. I have no doubt that I've woken some woodland creatures from their slumbers. I leave the gate open to avoid any other commotion that might attract attention to myself.

The path continues forward for a few steps through more heavy woods before it takes a sharp turn and opens up onto what looks to be a garden terrace in winter disguise. A large house looms behind it with a sagging roof and gnarled gables. The building looks Victorian and is painted a dark blue that might have appeared black had the sky not been bright with falling flurries. I count up the windows and a cellar opening to see that the house is three floors plus an attic and basement space. On one of the upper floors, an orange glow appears in one of the windows before quickly disappearing. Someone must be upstairs with a candle. It wouldn't be a surprise if the power has gone out considering the wind.

"It's so wonderful to see you again. It's Emma, isn't it?"

I startle at the sound of the voice. Behind me stands an elderly woman. Her hair is woven back into a bun with small, white whisps slipping out the sides to frame her pale face and large green eyes. She wears a dark scarf that matches her irises and has a snake-like pattern sewn into the knit fabric. She smiles at me, and the edges of her eyes turn down just enough so that the crow's feet framing each side of her face deepen into worn crevasses. She grabs my hands in hers. She isn't wearing any gloves, but a subtle warmth still presses into my fingers as her hands cling onto mine. A small emerald gem sits on her left ring finger.

"When last I saw you, you were barely walking." As she speaks, she stares into my eyes. They seem to be watering ever so slightly. The woman must be my Great Aunt Lois. I wonder how long she's been out in the cold waiting for me to arrive.

I hesitate before making a reply, unable to remember what the appropriate response is for greeting a relative I haven't seen since I was a toddler. I've paused too long though because Great Aunt Lois seems to know exactly what I'm thinking.

"You probably barely remember me from so long ago. Since we're both adults, why don't you just call me Lois? No need to worry about that Aunt Lois nonsense." The warmth radiating off of Lois's hands tingles up my arms and into my chest at her greeting. "Now, let's go get your suitcase from the car. I presume you parked it in the lane?"

She guides me towards the walking path that I ventured from earlier. Lois swiftly makes her way in the icy conditions with strong footing. She's wearing a thin coat that moves ever so slightly when she does. We arrive at my car, and I open the trunk to grab my suitcase out of it.

"You really should lock your doors," Lois says. "Even out here, you can never be too careful."

I give her a gentle smile in thanks for the friendly advice, but we are interrupted by a great gust of wind. A sound rumbles behind me, shaking the ground ever so slightly and causing the nearby trees to shed tiny membranes of snow. A huge tree branch, one of the limbs from a black walnut, has fallen to the ground. No doubt it had been weighed down by ice and pushed over by the heavy wind.

"Just a rotten branch, that's all," Lois says. She stares into the darkness of the forest for a moment.

"Does that type of thing happen a lot?" I ask.

"It depends what you mean," she answers.

Her eyes are on the spot where the tree branch crashed to the earth. I look back at the ancient limb. A large crack runs through the middle of the wood as if it had been struck by lightning at some point. Past the fallen branch, shadows of other trees move in the wind against the pale ground. The farther I look, the more the shadows blur together like one mass of darkness.

Lois leads me inside her house through a large, oak door painted midnight black. There's a pair of silver knockers in the center of the door—silver nuthatches, to be exact. The front foyer floor is covered in dark wood that stretches past the entrance into other rooms and halls that can be seen from near the doorway. On a side table, a purple candle burns, giving off a gentle scent of pine that is struggling to cover the heavy air's odor of must.

"I hope you don't mind the dark," Lois turns to me. "We always seem to lose the power when it's windy."

"I'm just happy to be here. I still can't believe I know the owner of *Nuthatch Nest!*"

"Let me show you up to your room. The stairs are through here."

Lois beckons me towards a twisting staircase with a thick banister that lacks any dust. The stairs are old enough that the centers of each step curve into discolored, shallow hollows. She takes me up to the second floor and down a narrow hallway before stopping at a green door with a brassy handle.

"I've always liked this room. It's always felt a little warmer to me than the others."

She pushes open the door and reveals a simple looking guest room accompanied with a double bed that's decorated with a dark green quilt to match a pair of heavy curtains. In the corner, a large wardrobe is positioned. Not counting the bed, it's the only piece of furniture in the room other than a small nightstand with an antique, milk glass lamp on top of it.

"This is great. Thank you so much," I say.

A high-pitched whistle breaks into the room and rattles the window. Lois smiles at me and giggles. Her laugh tickles my ears, and the hair on my arms stand up. "Old houses always complain about the wind." She heads toward the door but turns back right before she leaves. "We'll all be having dinner in about an hour. Why don't you get settled, and when you're ready, meet us downstairs?" She abruptly shuts the door, and I'm alone in the room.

Us? When I had originally spoken to Lois, she made it sound as if she lived alone. Maybe she has a live-in maid or someone who stays in the house to help her? I imagine taking care of a property this size isn't the easiest thing. I shake off the feeling, reminding myself to be thankful that I have this story to write about in the first place. Half the writers I work with would kill to have an inside scoop on *Nuthatch Nest*.

I take a moment to decompress. The wind is still rattling the window on and off, letting whistles fill the room. I reach for my phone to give Mr. Hawking a call so that he knows I've arrived at *Nuthatch Nest*, only to see that I don't have service. I shouldn't be surprised given the remote location of Lois's house. I'll check the service in some of the other rooms, or maybe I can borrow Lois's landline after dinner—that is if it still works without the power. I haven't used a landline since high school and can't exactly remember if they still work in outages.

Another gust of wind punches the window. I move aside one of the long, velvet curtains to peak outside. The room faces the gated path that I journeyed on earlier in the evening. The whole back of the house is surrounded by a thick wood. I imagine the birds are all snuggled away in their nests along with the squirrels and anything else that lives in the woods around the house. There's enough snow on the ground to create a brightness that makes the woods seem like shadows against an otherwise never-ending white backdrop. Some of the shadowy trees move in the wind, swaying back and forth silently. The winter mirage is interrupted when a shadow in the shape of a person appears near the back gate before it disappears into the woods. I try to track it, but the trees' shadows make it too difficult. Maybe Lois went down to lock her gate? The incident reminds me of the fallen tree near my car earlier. Lois had let her eyes settle past me as if she had been looking at something, and now, I can't help but wonder if she had seen a person.

The chill from standing so close to the window starts to settle under my skin. I take a step back and unpack my suitcase. I'm sure whatever I saw was nothing. While Lois is out in the middle of nowhere, that doesn't mean she doesn't have neighbors who might check on her property once in a while. I unzip my luggage and only take a few outfits out and my toiletries. The nightstand by the bed is so small that I decide to check the wardrobe to see if it might have some shelving for my things. Unfortunately, the doors of the large piece of furniture won't budge. There's a small keyhole near one of the handles that must be keeping it closed. Maybe Lois still uses it for storage. I go ahead and put everything back in my suitcase for the time being.

CHAPTER TWO

THE OTHER RESIDENTS

It hasn't been ten minutes since Lois left, let alone an hour, but I change into the thickest sweater I have in my suitcase along with my winter coat. Had I known that the house would be so cold, I would've brought warmer clothes to avoid dressing like a winter marshmallow.

I pull out an old birdwatching book and flip through some of the pages to an entry on the white-breasted nuthatch. For the last issue of "The Backyard Bird Blurb," Mr. Hawking had assigned me to write a whole article on the loggerhead shrike and their grasshopper hunting instincts. Researching grasshopper species all day wasn't exactly the type of exciting journalism I had once dreamt of pursuing. This opportunity to write about *Nuthatch Nest* is the first time that I've been given the chance to sculpt a big article. I have so many questions I want to ask Lois about the house. Despite *Nuthatch Nest's* renown name, the information available about it on the internet is pretty scarce.

I figure I could go downstairs and help her prepare dinner since there's not much else to do in my room. Outside in the hallway, it's notably warmer, and I'm finally reprieved of the sound of the wind. The hall is decorated in mustard yellow wallpaper with floral accents. Every so often, an old painting hangs between doors. Most of the art is nature scenes of forests, ponds, or gardens. I stop and study one of the works that's a few doors down from my room and is slightly different from the others. The sky is painted using dark purples, and a lake swirled with blue and green is embellished below it. In the picture, two dogs huddle near a group of trees.

"That's one of my favorites."

I jump at the voice.

"I didn't mean to startle you." A man who looks to be in his early fifties with black hair lightly streaked with silver has appeared in the hallway. His dark eyes glint as he speaks, looking like polished onyx.

"I thought you might've been lost in the hallway." He extends a hand out to me. "I'm Charlie Kim, one of Lois's boarders, or housemates. That might be a better word."

Everything starts to make a little more sense. The shadows in the woods, Lois using the word "we" when she talked about dinner—she rents out her rooms in the house. Of course, Lois wouldn't be living in this giant house all alone out in the country. There's no way she would live comfortably while trying to take care of all these rooms and the surrounding property that looks like it goes on for miles.

"I'm Emma, Lois's great niece. It's nice to meet you," I say.

"I thought that's who you might be. Lois is so excited to have family visiting. She's been talking up a storm about you. She's stuck seeing the same faces every day, so a visitor like you is a true novelty."

"Who are the others?"

"The other people who live here with Lois. You didn't think she lived in this house all by herself, did you?"

"I didn't know," I say.

Charlie gives me a hearty laugh. "I can't imagine living in this house all by myself."

"I can't imagine living in it at all." My cheeks warm as soon as the words are out of my mouth. "That's not what I meant! It's a beautiful house. It's just different from what I imagined. It's darker and colder than I thought it would be."

Charlie smiles at my rambling. "Don't let the storm ruin your impression of the old place. I know it looks a tad spooky now, but in the summer, the gardens at the back of the house are spectacular, and the woods make you feel like you live in another world. I wouldn't live anywhere else."

"That's good to hear. I'm sure I'll get used to it in no time."

"There are very few houses like this left in the area with such a unique history."

"I can't wait to learn more about it," I say.

Charlie gestures to the painting I had been studying. "This painting of the dogs is my favorite. It's actually one of the newest ones in this hallway. I'm sure you'll meet Rockey and Rodeo soon enough. I should warn you though, they're a bit peculiar when it comes to showing affection."

"Rockey and Rodeo?"

"The two dogs in the painting. Those are Lois's. Lois loves her animals and her ice cream. Don't be surprised if you hear some bumps in the night. That's when the dogs are most active."

Charlie glances down at his watch before peering back up at me. "Dinner is soon, so I better get going. The dining room is just down the stairs and to the left of the entrance." Charlie smiles at me before he heads down the hall and disappears.

After giving the painting of the dogs a last cursory glance, I make my way downstairs by using the tightly wound staircase until I'm back in the foyer. The candle from earlier is still lit, sending flickering flame shadows across the wall. The foyer is much colder than it was earlier in the evening, and I can't help but hope that the dining room will be a bit warmer. Off to the left of the entrance and through a large, arching doorway, candles are lit on a sideboard, creating a hum of soft light. I figure this must be the dining room.

Inside the room, the deep scent of basil and rose mix together. The little blazes from the candles scattered around the room lick the air as if they are trying to taste the aromas coming from the kitchen. Two large bookshelves line the back walls of the room. The books appear dusty as if no one has bothered to read them in some time. In the center of the room, the dining room table stretches out like a dark shadow trying to snuff out the candle flames. It's made of a black wood and is surrounded by chairs with deep green cushions detailed with silver upholstery tacks. The table is set with matching green placemats and silver cutlery, but otherwise, it sits empty. Charlie hasn't arrived yet despite leaving before me.

Lois bustles into the room from the doorway wearing a completely different outfit from earlier in the day. She has loosely wrapped a dark blue pashmina over her shoulders, and a large, matching blue pendant now hangs from her neck. She glances in my direction before pursing her lips and taking a seat at the table. I smile in her direction, but she turns her head, purposefully ignoring me.

"Does it matter which seat I take?" I ask.

"Why would I mind?" she says back while refusing to look at me.

I sit down in a seat diagonally across from her. An awkward air seems to cling to our presence, a much cooler tone from the earlier welcoming warmth Lois provided me when I first met her on the walking path. I glance around the table. It could probably seat 10, but it is set for five, with one person sitting at the head. I know that one of the remaining seats will be taken by Charlie, but I have no idea who the other two dinner guests will be.

"Thank you so much for letting me stay here," I start the conversation back up again.

Lois leans forward across the table, and her blue pendant sparkles against some of the silverware. "I didn't have a say in the matter," she smugly replies before turning her head away from me a second time.

Lois shifts in her seat before reaching up to play with her necklace. She wears a matching silver and blue bracelet on her wrist. I think about complimenting her on her jewelry to lighten the mood when another figure appears in the doorway. She looks to be around the same age as Lois. She has dark, curly locks that have been tied back into a bun with just a few strands left out to frame her face. Her round eyes are a deep brown color and are sunken far into her face, unlike her cheekbones that stick out prominently, with just the slightest touch of rouge, and her freckles that dot her dark skin.

"I love company," the stranger comes over to the table before draping her arm over my chair and taking a seat next to me. Up close, I can see the edges of gray roots growing in under her hair. "Emma, right?"

"Yes," I nod my head.

"Wonderful to meet you. I'm Bernice." Her voice is deep and toned as if she practices talking. "I was so excited when Lois told me you were coming."

"Of course, you were," Lois replies across the table with another smug look.

Bernice rolls her eyes. "Don't mind her. She never liked your Great Uncle Albert. She thinks anyone related to him can't be any good to have around," she says in a voice that is supposed to sound like a whisper but is clearly loud enough for Lois to hear.

I nod politely at Bernice's comment, still trying to understand why Lois agreed to have me here if she hates all of her late husband's relatives. Lois ignores the both of us, mindlessly playing with her necklace as she waits for dinner to begin. This doesn't seem to bother Bernice though.

"I heard you'll be writing about the house for a magazine. How exciting, a single girl with her own job and own independence. It reminds me of when I was your age. All that freedom and the dates and dinners—getting asked out by so many dashing men," Bernice says.

"That's only because they knew you wouldn't say no," Lois quips.

"I don't think that was the only reason." Bernice smiles at me and winks. Her eyes move to something behind me. "Here she is! Lois, don't you look darling?"

I turn around and see Lois standing in the doorway. She's wearing the same green scarf as earlier with the accompanying green ring. I quickly glance between the Lois standing in the doorway and the Lois sitting at the table.

The Lois in green smiles at Bernice's comments. "Thank you. I see you've been talking to my niece. Hopefully only good things?" She sits down next to her doppelganger. Immediately, I can't help but notice the difference in their facial dispositions. "Emma, Bernice is one of my oldest friends. She lives here with me and my sister, Madge."

"That makes sense," I blurt before a burst of blush tickles my cheeks. "I thought Madge was you."

Lois laughs. "I'll take that as a compliment. Madge is two years younger. When we were around your age, we didn't look as much alike, but as we got older, things seemed to change."

Madge's only reaction to this comment is to raise her eyebrows. While the two sisters look alike, their personalities couldn't be any more different.

"I might've forgotten to mention that I have boarders living here when I talked with you on the phone about staying here and writing an article," Lois says. "I own the house, but I can't stand the thought of all these rooms sitting empty and unused. Bernice moved in around the time Albert passed, and my other boarder, Charlie, moved in about a year ago. Madge and I have lived together since we were little, even when Albert was here."

Madge's face seems to darken at the mention of Albert, and her fingers faulter as she continues to play with her jewelry.

"Lois, how exactly are you and Emma related?" Bernice asks, changing the conversation back to me and easing the tension.

Madge rolls her eyes before Lois starts to talk. "Well, I married Albert, and he had seven sisters and four brothers, the oldest being named Gene, who would be Emma's grandfather."

"I always wanted to be from a big family," Bernice says, "but it's always just been little old me and Lois. She's like family to me." Her eyes catch on the light as they give a quick flick towards Madge. "And Madge too," she mutters.

"After Albert died," Lois continues, "this house just felt so lonely, so naturally, I asked Bernice to come join me.

"I was still around," Madge mumbles in the direction of her dinner plate.

"I've always needed lots of company," Lois says. "Albert was such a gem to have around too. He was the type of person whose absence was really felt." Her eyes wander past mine towards the wall behind me in a similar fashion to how they did when the tree branch outside had fallen near my car.

"You know, right after I got here, my mom told me the most ridiculous stories about Great Uncle Albert. She seemed to think he was a detective or something."

"Wouldn't that have been fun?" Madge smiles and deep lines paint themselves around her eyes, making her look rather wolfish.

Lois gives a hollow laugh. "That would've been something, but no, he was just a retired banker by the time I met him. We married a bit later in life."

There's a commotion on the other side of the room, and Charlie appears with a large pot in his oven-wrapped hands. "Right out of the oven! Just kidding. I made it earlier today, and at the exact moment we lost power, I pulled it out of the oven so that it could cool. It's still pretty warm."

Lois's smile brightens. "Usually, I do the cooking since meals are included in the rent and board, but once in a while Charlie gets an itch, and he'll cook every meal for a whole week! I was hesitant when a man wanted to rent a room, but I don't regret saying yes to him."

"I think he's rather cute too," Bernice whispers in my ear before giving me another wink. This time, she actually manages to whisper without anyone else hearing.

The five of us settle into our dinners. The food warms my stomach, reminding me that I haven't eaten much today. Charlie really is a great cook. The spices he's used prick at my tongue at the same time as sweetening it.

"Emma, what type of magazine do you work for?" Bernice asks.

"I work for a magazine called *The Binocular Feather Feature Birding Magazine*, but most people just refer to it as the "The BFF Birding Magazine." Our ideal reader is someone who enjoys birds and reading."

Bernice nods her head and smiles at me. "It sounds quite quaint."

"The names a mouthful," Madge mutters. "It sounds like a real mess."

I ignore Madge and continue, "I'm responsible for writing "The Backyard Bird Blurb." For each issue, I usually write about a common bird that our readers might spot in their own backyards, usually a songbird, and I give tips to our readers to help spot them. The article I'm working on about *Nuthatch Nest* is more front-page material, at least, that's the hope." The heat returns to my face, and I know it's not because I've bitten into something spicy.

"A writer of the natural world," Bernice says. "Writing must run in the family. I bet you didn't know that your Aunt Lois and I were both writers. Quite famous too."

The lines that frame Lois's small mouth move a hint upward. "We had pen names of course, so you might not have known. Bernice makes us sound much more interesting than we are."

"Nonsense, we really were big. We wrote gothics together. You know the type, big houses, spooky evenings, true love. Nothing beats a gothic. They even made a few movies out of the books we wrote together. They were a smash."

"They weren't the only things that were smashed," Madge mumbles under her breath.

Bernice's eye dart over the table. "What did you say?"

Madge ignores her and continues eating as if Bernice isn't at the table. Earlier, Bernice had playfully pushed away Madge's comments, but now, judging from the sparks behind her brown eyes, Bernice isn't having any of it.

"Madge, you always were an ungrateful—"

The rest of her words are cut off by a loud knock on the door.

Chapter Three

VISITORS

"Who could that be?" Charlie says, breaking the tension.

Bernice slips her eyes away from Madge. "Were you expecting another guest, Lois?"

"No," Lois replies as she folds her napkin on the table.

"You ladies stay here then, and I'll get it," Charlie volunteers before leaving the room.

"I can't even remember the last time I heard anyone knock on that door," Lois says.

"I don't think anyone ever has until now," quips Madge.

Everyone at the table has stopped eating and seems to be sitting in a suspended realm of air. I had thought the disagreement between Madge and Bernice had been awkward, but this silence is much worse. Madge's eyes pierce the doorframe that leads into the foyer. From where I sit, I can hear Charlie opening the heavy door followed by some low murmurs. The sound of the door closing and multiple footsteps on the floorboards pricks my ears.

"It seems like we're going to have more company," Lois says.

Madge glares at me across the table as if I'm the one who invited the mysterious party guests and ruined her night. I give her an uncomfortable smile before studying the silverware set on the table before me. I can't be more thankful to be sitting next to Bernice instead of her. How could she and Lois be so close with one another? One so welcoming and the other so miserable?

The suspended realm of air around us breaks as the silhouette of a body slices through the archway, the shadow sucking away the light like spoiled wine attracting fruit flies. A woman steps out of the darkness and reveals herself. Her pale hair is pulled back in a tight French twist so that her face bears no wrinkles, at least not any that I can see. She smiles at us sitting around the table. I can't discern her age for certain, but she looks to be only a few years older than myself.

"Am I disturbing anything?" she asks. Her voice is high and delicate. "I got into a little accident up on the road with all the wind, and now I can't get my car to start. I also forgot my cell phone at home, which is so typical of me. Always being mindless."

Lois stands up to greet her. "That certainly is a lot of trouble to go through on a night like this! Please, take a seat at the table."

Madge's face quickly loses color and turns pale as the new guest sits down. She looks like she might be ill. I've known Madge for less than an hour, and her dislike for newcomers is already apparent.

The stranger's eyes warm. "You can't imagine how thankful I am to get out of that wind outside. I've never felt anything like it before."

"The lane to the house is so long. You must be exhausted coming all the way from the main road!" Lois says.

"It was a walk," the visitor says, "but I wasn't alone. The man who I got in the accident with came with me. We tried using his cellphone to call for help, but there was no reception. We made our way down your drive, hoping to come across a house." Her cheeks are flushed a pretty pink from the cold outside. She appears rather flustered and embarrassed to be intruding on our dinner party. "My name's Natalie. I hope it's alright that I stay here for a bit."

"Certainly," Lois says. "No one should be out and about with gales like these."

"What happened to the driver of the other car in the accident?" Bernice asks. "You said he came with you?"

"The man who answered the door took him to the kitchen to use the telephone." Natalie's eyes land on the food sitting on the table. Wisps of steam still rise off of it in the chilly air of the dining room.

"Would you like a bite? I'm sure you must be famished after the hike to the house. We always have enough food to share," Lois says. She grabs a spare plate that Charlie had brought in earlier and scoops a helping onto it.

"That would be wonderful," Natalie says, her eyes light up.

As Natalie takes her first bite, the doorway darkens with a new shadow. Standing right where Natalie's silhouette had been just moments ago is a young man. His hair, a medium brown color with hues of auburn, matches his eyes and is smoothed back. It looks wet, most likely from the snow flurries outside. His lips are chapped a light peach from the cold, and his cheeks are pinched pink as well. He glances at the group of us sitting at the table before he notices me staring. I avert my eyes back to the half-eaten dinner on my plate as my hand unconsciously pats my hair, preening my wild, dark blonde curls and patting flyaways.

He gives a light knock on the wall, gaining the attention of the rest of the women sitting at the table. "I'm so sorry for intruding like this. I'm sure Natalie told you that we got in a fender-bender over on the road, and there was no reception. Your friend Charlie let me use the telephone. I just wanted to let Natalie know it was free now in case she wanted to call anyone."

"That would be perfect actually," Natalie stands up from the table to go and join the man.

"I'll come with you, Natalie," Lois says. "It's an old rotary phone, and some people find it a bit tricky."

It's now just me, Madge, and Bernice at the table. Charlie has yet to come back. Madge's mouth is pinched, and she continues to avoid my eyes by staring intently at her bracelet. Bernice, on the other hand, leans towards me, her deep brown eyes not shying away from mine.

"What a strange dinner this is turning out to be," she grabs my arm playfully.

"This room doesn't feel right," Madge says suddenly.

Bernice rolls her eyes. "Nothing ever feels right to you."

Madge stares at her blankly before getting up and leaving the room.

"She's always been like that. I know Lois and her are sisters, but I still can't figure out why Lois ever puts up with her. Lois gives her the world, and Madge acts like she's owed it." Bernice pushes out of her chair. "Now that the food is getting cold so am I. I'll be right back. I just want to grab a cardigan."

Bernice leaves me alone in the room. It is a bit cooler than it was earlier. My hands in particular feel like their filled with cold sludge instead of warm blood. I'm hoping that the comforter on my bed will be able to keep me warm tonight.

Natalie reenters the dining room followed by Lois and Harry.

"If this isn't a bad day, I don't know what is," Natalie says before letting out a sigh. "Both the towing company and the insurance agents say it's a lost cause to come out here tonight because of the wind. Our cars aren't blocking the road, so they're not a high-level hazard. All the available crews are on full alert trying to restart power in the town and clear roads."

"The two of you can stay here then," Lois offers. "We have enough bedrooms." I wonder if the other rooms are as barren as mine or if they contain more furnishings.

"Thank you so much," Harry says before taking a seat next to me at the table. He smiles in my direction as he shrugs off his coat and loops it around the back of his chair. Up close, I can see where the snow has melted in his hair and formed small water droplets.

It's at that moment that we are all shaken by a scream.

CHAPTER FOUR

A FALL IN THE KITCHEN

Madge appears in the doorway, her face as pale as the dinner plates in front of us. "It's Charlie! Something is wrong!"

"What do you mean?" Bernice appears behind her, her hands fiddling with a button on her cardigan.

"I found him in the kitchen—just lying there! When I tried to talk to him, he didn't move."

Harry springs up next to me.

"I think we all better go see," Lois says.

I hope that Charlie has just taken a fall and is only temporarily knocked out. When we arrive in the kitchen, Charlie is lying on the floor, glassware and pottery smashed in pieces around him like an ancient mosaic. I can see a few drops of what I can only assume to be blood spotted across some of the floor. A warmth spreads through the heart of my stomach and travels up my body, making me feel queasy.

Harry kneels down and grabs his wrist, taking his pulse. He seems to wait a few seconds before looking up at all of us.

"I think he just took a bad fall," Harry says.

"Is he going to be okay?" I ask.

"We'll have to see when he wakes up, but he isn't dead."

Harry shifts Charlie's body so that the older man is on his side, and his head is tilted towards the floor. As he does so, Charlie stirs slightly and groans.

"What happened?" he asks and blinks against the dim candlelight of the kitchen.

"It looks like you took a spill," Harry says. "You might not want to stand up too fast."

"Who are you?" asks Charlie. "And who is she?" he's now looking in my direction as he speaks.

There's a clanging sound as Bernice places the telephone handset into the receiver on the kitchen wall. "The phone has just gone out, probably from the storm. There's no way to call for an ambulance now."

"What about our cellphones?" I pull out mine from my pocket to see that it has no signal.

"Call me old fashioned, but Lois, Madge, and I never got around to getting cellular devices, and when Charlie first moved in, he checked every room in the house for a signal to no avail," say Bernice. "Without the landline, we're as good as shipwrecked."

"We better get him up to bed," Lois says. "What awful timing."

Harry helps Charlie stagger to his feet until he's standing. He takes a few steps by himself before he gets the hang of it.

"I should help him to his room," Lois says to Harry before she whisks Charlie out of the room.

I'm hoping Charlie doesn't live on the top floor. He might have trouble navigating all those flights up the tight stairwell.

"How did he end up on the floor, Madge?" asks Bernice.

Madge turns a cold look towards Bernice. "How am I to know?" she says. "He was on the floor when I found him."

"You didn't see how he fell?"

"I would've told you if I saw how he fell," Madge snaps. "I said I found him on the floor. I didn't say I saw how he got there."

"I think I need a moment to myself," Bernice says. "I'm not used to all this commotion. I'll be in my room if anyone needs me."

"Me too," Madge echoes. "I don't care to be interrogated in my own home."

The two women leave the room followed by Natalie who is in search of the powder room. I glance over at Harry now that we're left alone. He's leaning against the kitchen counter with his arms crossed so that the muscles in his forearms are taut. He twitches his wrist, and the face of his watch flashes in the candlelight. It has a pale purple face, and I see the time is well past nine, much later than I had realized.

"Good thing you were here to help," I say. "I don't know if any of us would've known what to do without you. Are you a doctor or a nurse?"

Harry smiles. "No, I just coach my nephew's little league team and happen to be first-aid certified. I actually work for a detective agency."

"A detective agency?" The words fly out of my mouth while my mind conjures up a random image of Sherlock Holmes on a cruise ship, reminding me of my earlier conversation with my mother about Great Uncle Albert.

"I work in the accounting department, so I'm not a detective myself. The most exciting thing that I get to do is go through the company write-offs. Those are kind of fun." He smiles and little shallows appear under his cheeks. "What about you?"

"I write for a magazine. I'm Emma by the way." Heat spreads across my hands and neck as his eyes look into mine. "I'm actually here to write an article about the house. I work for a birding magazine, and this house was built for the daughter of a famous ornithologist. Lois also happens to be my great aunt, so I got the exclusive scoop."

Harry doesn't seem to notice my flush. Instead, his eyes kindly follow along as I talk. "It is a very unique home. I couldn't believe how fortunate I was that this house was here. I thought for sure I'd be walking for a few miles before I could get help after the fender-bender I had with Natalie."

"This old house sure is something. It's just a bit spookier than I thought."

As soon as the words leave my mouth, a thud rings out from the dining room.

CHAPTER FIVE

DEATH IN THE DINING ROOM

"Lois!" I cry out. She's lying on the floor next to the dining room table. The great slab of wood looks like a dark coffin reaching out and grasping the living light from my great aunt. Her poor body is crumpled into distortion, and her skin is so gray that she resembles an old, discarded newspaper.

"Lois!" I cry again, hoping she'll wake up. I have no idea what has happened. First Charlie fell in the kitchen, and now, Lois is lying on the floor of the dining room within a span of what feels like less than ten minutes.

"What is it, darling?" A voice asks from behind me. Lois has appeared in the doorway wearing the same dark green scarf from earlier. She puts a hand to her mouth and releases an audible gasp. "Madge!"

The woman on the floor has a blue pashmina wrapped around her frail shoulders and a large blue pendant tangled in the wisps of her white hair. It isn't Lois who is on the floor, but rather, her doppelganger sister, Madge.

Natalie and Bernice come rushing into the room.

Natalie's eyes widen in shock. "Is she okay?"

"How could this have happened?" Lois gets on her knees and gently rubs her sister's arm. She pulls her sister towards her, and the room seems to darken on its own accord. On the left side of Madge's neck is a long, red cut. A steak knife lies just underneath her.

A pale shadow crosses over Lois's face and sucks the warmth out of it. "She's dead."

"We need to call for help!" Natalie says frantically as her blue eyes grow even wider than before.

"The lines are dead," Harry says.

"What do we do?" Natalie's voice has gone up an octave.

Lois's mouth seems to be repeating something in a small whisper. It's a moment before I can hear her words over the commotion. "Is she really dead?"

"Oh dear," says Bernice quietly. She goes over and pulls Lois away from her sister's body. "Come to the kitchen, Lois," she says in a soothing voice. "No good can come of us staying in here."

Lois drifts from the floor with the help of her friend. Her movement is spectral and trancelike as Bernice leads her away. Harry and I follow them, not wanting to be left alone in the dining room after such an event.

Bernice picks up the housephone and holds it against her ear for a good few seconds before she sets it back into its cradle. With the power out, the phone lines out, and the road being unnavigable, the walls of Lois's grand house are starting to feel like they're squeezing tight around my chest.

"I feel sick," Lois says as one of her limp hands dabs at her dewy forehead.

The rest of the remaining guests have gathered in the kitchen except for Charlie who is resting upstairs. Natalie hovers by the oven, no doubt trying to absorb as much heat from the appliance as possible. Lois sits on a stool next to a nearby window decorated in happy yellow curtains that don't fit the mood, and Harry is pacing back and forth in front of the refrigerator.

"First Charlie and now Madge," Lois's voice comes out empty. Her eyes are wet and glassy with the threat of tears.

"Whoever did it is in the house," Bernice says, her voice deep and dark. She eyes me before she turns away. Her friendliness from earlier disappearing like all the heat in the room.

"That doesn't mean it's one of us though," says Harry.

"What do you mean?" I ask.

"It's a big house. Someone could've snuck in and escaped, or they could still be here hiding. Who knows?"

I think back to the shadow I thought I saw earlier in the day. Had that been an intruder? Someone slipping into the house with malice in their mind? I shiver at the thought.

"Should we check to see if any doors are open or windows smashed?" I ask.

Lois shakes her head. "We never lock the doors around here. Usually, no one is around. We keep the cellar, a backdoor, and the front door all unlocked." She pauses. "I would've locked them if I had known something like this would happen. This is all my fault for not locking them. Madge's dead because of me."

"Don't say that, Lois," Bernice rubs her shoulder gently. "This was in no way your fault."

"Whoever did it could still be in here though," I say. "Shouldn't we at least check?"

"No," Bernice says firmly from her spot in the kitchen, ice still in her eyes. "We should all go to our rooms, and lock the doors, and wait for Charlie to wake up. Whoever hit Charlie must've killed Madge. He'll remember who hit him once he has some rest. We'll also lock the dining room door so that no one disturbs the body."

"How will Charlie know where we all are when he wakes up?" Harry asks.

"We'll write a note and leave it on his nightstand. We'll all put it there together and leave together. That way no one can try anything," Bernice says. "If he doesn't wake up within two hours, we'll all go and check on him at the same time."

We're all stunned by the night's revelations and exhausted by the hour, so the lot of us concede to the plan without question. Together, we write a short note explaining the unfortunate situation before leaving for Charlie's bedroom. As we ascend the stairs, I can't help but feel a pair of eyes boring into my back.

Once we all leave the note in Charlie's room and go our separate ways, I reach my own room and pull out my phone from my pocket before tucking it into the suitcase. There's no point in carrying around a phone when I can't get reception.

I peer out the window to see the snow whip left and right, making the flakes look like New Year's confetti. Unlike confetti though, most of it disappears before it hits the ground. I haven't seen any shadows since earlier in the evening, but I can't help but feel like I'm being watched. Although, everyone is watching everyone at this point. No one in the house can be trusted except Harry, who was with me when we heard the thump of Madge falling to her demise, and technically Madge, who didn't attack herself.

A light knock sounds on my door. "It's Harry, can I come in?"

I hesitate before lightly opening the door and beckoning him inside. Harry's wearing a blue fleece over his shirt and a pair of light-colored jeans. His hair is a shade brighter than earlier in the evening when it was still wet with the remnants of snowflakes. It's a pleasing brown color that contrasts nicely with his pink-pinched cheeks. If we had met somewhere else like a coffee shop, I would probably be pining for him to ask me on a date, but I don't find the circumstances of murder to be the most romantic ones, and I would hope that Harry would agree with that sentiment.

Harry takes a seat on my bed and runs a hand through his hair and gives it a little ruffle in the process. "Sorry for bothering you, but I need to talk things through with someone about what happened," he says.

A breath of air escapes my lips as if it's been trapped inside a tomb. "I feel the same. I don't know what we were thinking, agreeing to all sit in our rooms alone right after we had found Madge. We all must've been in a bit of shock."

"Exactly." Harry pauses after the word, letting it hang in the air. "There's nothing worse than just sitting in our rooms and waiting for the next strike. I know this will sound crazy, but it doesn't seem like help is on the way soon, and my gut is telling me to get ahead of the murderer before things get worse."

Harry looks up at me.

I meet his eyes in silence.

He doesn't say anything, so I talk next. "Are you suggesting that we try to figure out who murdered Madge?"

Harry gives me a simple nod.

"I'm a writer, not a detective. I don't think I'm qualified in the least to solve a murder."

There's a short pause before I speak again. "If we do anything, it should be figuring out another way to go for help. We know the phones don't work, and driving is out of the question with the debris that'll be all over the road from the wind, but maybe one of us could go for help on foot? I know no one else lives nearby, but it couldn't hurt—"

My words are cut off by the wind as it hurls itself against the window with such strength that a loud crack echoes through the room. A thin line now runs from the top of the pane to the bottom where a pebble has been lodged into the glass.

"If the wind is strong enough to be cracking windows with small rocks, I don't think it's a smart idea for anyone to leave the house," says Harry.

"I guess you're right," I say.

Harry stands up off the bed and gently holds my hands in his firm ones. "I know neither of us knows what we're doing, but we need to look at the scenario we're in. Someone in this house killed Madge less than two hours ago, and as far as I can see, we're all sitting ducks until the police come, or someone figures out who did it. With the storm the way it is and the power and the phones out, we either sit around with our fingers crossed, or we try and do something until help gets here." He ends his speech with a pleading look that makes me realize that it's taken a lot of courage for him to come here and say this to me.

I had been so caught up in Madge's murder that I hadn't thought about the fact that everyone still in the house could be in danger. Whoever killed Madge could have been targeting her, or they could be after something in this house and unafraid to hurt anyone who gets in their way. Or worse, they could be after multiple people and determined to work their way through everyone. A great heaviness settles on my chest like a ghostly hand pushing into my lungs. I know I don't know Lois well, but she is my family, and part of me knows the right thing to do would be to protect her and prevent what happened to Madge from happening to her.

"This sounds like we're trapped in a murder mystery novel," I say.

"Let's at least talk it through," he says.

"Well, there are—were— seven of us until Madge died. We know it's not Madge, and we know it's not you or me because we were both in the kitchen together. That leaves four possibilities: Bernice, Lois, Natalie, and Charlie."

"And the fifth possibility that it was an outsider," says Harry. "Lois said they never lock their doors.

"Earlier tonight, before dinner, I did see some shadows out in the forest. I guess that could point to an intruder."

Harry nods his head. "Okay, this is good. Now we just need to think of motives."

"Bernice and Madge got in a fight right before you and Natalie got here." I tell him about their terse exchange at the dinner table.

"Bernice definitely has a motive then. I'm tempted to cross Natalie off because we just met up at the road, so I don't see how she would even know Madge."

"She could've been trying to steal something and got caught?"

"Why would she stick around though?"

"True," I say. "I also don't think it was Lois. When I first met Madge, she was upset that Lois had invited me to be a guest, but that doesn't sound like a strong motive when it comes to murder. They're also sisters who have lived together forever, why kill her now?"

"So that leaves Charlie, but he was knocked out in the kitchen."

"Not when Madge was killed though. In fact, Madge was the one that found Charlie in the kitchen. Maybe she saw who hurt Charlie? Or maybe she hurt Charlie somehow, and he went back to hurt her?"

We are both quiet for a moment while the wind bites against the window and howls into the room.

"I don't really see how any of this is helping. All we've done is ask ourselves a bunch of questions. This is just reaffirming the fact that I'm not a detective," I say.

"Look, I know we're not detectives, but we can't just let someone go around hurting all these people when we might be able to stop them. The only person I can trust in this house is you because you were with me when Madge was attacked. Please, I can't do this alone, and I also can't sit here doing nothing."

I bite my lip, and an uncomfortable warmth of nerves grows in my stomach. I know he's right about being sitting ducks. I've been bird-watching enough times in my life to know that being a sitting duck isn't a good thing. "Fine. I'll work with you but only because we need to make sure this person doesn't hurt anyone else."

Harry gives my hand a gentle squeeze in response. "We need to get more information out of everyone. We also need to look around the house to see if there are signs of a break-in. I know Lois doesn't lock her doors, but there could still be signs of an intruder. Let's scope out the house now while everyone is still in their rooms. We'll just have to make sure not to get caught." He runs his hand through his hair again, and I start to question my theory about murder mysteries and romance.

Chapter Six

THE LIBRARY

Harry and I both agree that the best place to start looking is the ground floor. It would be unlikely that an intruder penetrated the interior via the second floor or anything higher. Plus, as I pointed out to Harry, it would be easier to explore the downstairs areas than the upstairs. People might hear our creaking footsteps from the ceilings above, but it would be much more difficult to suspect we were wandering around below. We both agree that the trickiest part of our mission will be the hallway just outside my door. I'm not sure how many of the bedrooms on the second floor are in use, but it's safe to say I'm not the only one staying on this floor. The narrow hallway passes by three doors before it meets the spindly staircase Lois and I used just hours earlier. Harry has already informed me that the door closest to the stairs leads to his room, so we have to escape the eyes of two second floor dwellers before reaching our destination.

As we step out of my room, Harry is careful to close the door slowly by twisting the doorhandle in a meticulous manner so that not even a click sounds from the lock. Even without flashlights, we are able to make out a good bit of the hallway. Someone has left a collection of white candles lit on one of the sideboards. Wax drips off them and splatters onto the wood of the table like melting icicles. After a little bit of trial and error, we decide that shuffling our feet creates less noise than the unanticipated squawk of a floorboard that occurs even with the softest tippy toes. We make it past the room nearest to mine without issue. No light comes from the crack under the door, and we figure the room is empty, or the inhabitant must be asleep.

As we shuffle closer to the second door, it's apparent that someone is awake. A flickering orange light comes and goes underneath the crack in the door, and as we get closer, the murmur of low voices can be heard.

"We were so close," the one voice says, decisively female.

The other voice is too low to discern. I can't even tell if it's a man or a woman.

"We'll take care of it. That's for certain," the original voice replies.

Seconds pass as the room has grown quiet. Whatever conversation was happening is over now. Harry and I continue to shuffle towards the stairs, our socked feet making barely a sound against the wooden floor. Once we've made it down the stairs and find ourselves standing in the front foyer, we feel safe enough to talk.

"Could you make out what the voices were saying in the room?" he asks.

"Not anything useful. There were definitely two people in there though, so you and I aren't the only ones breaking the rules."

Harry takes out his cellphone and activates the flashlight app. "I don't have a ton of battery," he tells me. "But I should have enough for us to explore a couple of rooms. I didn't want to turn it on upstairs and risk someone seeing us."

We make our way to the kitchen, checking that the windows are all locked and that there are no other entry points. It was the scene of

Charlie's accident, after all. Other than a couple rooms on the ground floor, neither of us is familiar with the floorplan of Lois's house, so we decide to take a chance and wander down a hall that breaks off from the kitchen in the direction opposite of the dining room. The floor is covered in the same dark wood as the rest of the house but seems less inclined to squeak. The few flashes I see of the walls from Harry's phone show me that dark blue wallpaper with tiny forget-me-nots has been pasted floor to ceiling.

The first door we try in the hallway is a broom closet with nothing but dusty mops and cleaning supplies. The second door we open leads to a powder room that's even smaller than the closet. I make a mental note not to use that bathroom. The third door we try opens up to a large space with several incredible windows. Harry turns off his flashlight as the light from the snowy sky outside makes it easier to see. The room appears to be a library. The floor is decorated in plush rugs and has large armchairs positioned in the corner by the door. Bookshelves line the middle of the room so that it is difficult to see the other side of the library.

"It's a lot warmer in here," Harry says.

I notice it too. The freeze that had settled into my arms and legs doesn't seem as unbearable as it had been earlier in the night. We walk past the six or seven bookshelves until we find the reason why it's warmer. At the other end of the room, a dying fire crackles in front of a cushioned couch and a few more chairs.

"The fire looks like it was set a while ago. I doubt anyone has been in here recently," Harry says.

"It would've been nice if we'd all agreed to wait in here instead of our rooms. I can already feel myself defrosting."

Harry cracks a smile in my direction. His eyes give off the smallest twinkle from the fire, making them look almost orangey-red in the amber light. A sound of something cracking against wood sets us back into the moment.

"Maybe a book fell?" Harry looks doubtful.

We hear the crack again, but this time, it becomes rhythmic—occurring in several second intervals like a metronome.

I shake my head. "Definitely not a book. Books don't fall like that."

I make my way towards the sound. It's coming from somewhere deep in the maze of bookshelves where it is significantly darker than the rest of the room. Suddenly, my legs strike something soft, and I trip into the darkness and fall to the floor. Something wet and cold prods my neck, and I let out a scream. Harry's footsteps rush towards me, and he turns on his flashlight app before bursting into hushed laughs.

A dog stands over me, his nose curiously sniffing my face as his tail smacks against the bookcase. Another dog sits nearby, also wagging his tail.

"Rockey and Rodeo," I say, remembering my earlier conversation with Charlie. "Lois must keep her dogs in the library when she has guests. Which is why the fire was left going."

The two dogs appear to be black, curly haired mutts that look almost identical. I ponder the chances that they were taken from the same litter. The dog who greeted me with his nose has white patches on his front paws, and a saddle-shaped white marking on his back. He must be Rodeo.

"Emma, look," Harry whispers.

He's walked away from the dogs and is examining some large curtains near the fire. I give Rockey a pat that is much appreciated before I join Harry. He's pulled aside the curtains to show me that they are hiding not a window, but a pair of delicate French doors. Outside, the wind is working hard to blow around snow and cover up a set of deep footprints—coming and going from the house. It looks like Harry's theory about an intruder might not be so far-fetched after all.

CHAPTER SEVEN

I. WRIGHTER AND B. BOOKERTON

H arry and I make our way back upstairs. The footprints in the snow are strong evidence of an intruder. Now that we know Madge could've been hurt by an outsider, there's less reason for us to be suspicious of the others, and less reason for them to be suspicious of us. We slowly crack open the door to my room, hoping for a reprieve from having to sneak around when I let out a small yelp, my second of the day. Bernice is sitting on my bed with her arms crossed.

"I thought I heard someone prowling around. I heard you scream, so I came in here to check on you only to discover you were gone and had made a mess of the place." Her dark eyes dig into us. She's holding a flashlight that she places facing upward on the nightstand, giving the room ample amount of light.

I look around my tiny room and realize it's been turned upside down. The large wardrobe that was impenetrable earlier in the night has been forced open. Its contents are strewn everywhere. Old coats are lumped into messy piles, and shoes callously tossed across the space. Shirts askew on their hangers are huddled in corners, and dust floats quietly in the air.

"I didn't do this," I manage while heat climbs my neck.

"I should've listened to Madge when she said she didn't trust anyone from Albert's side of the family." Her voice is deep and decisive. "Obviously, you didn't find what you were looking for," she gestures to a medium sized wooden box on the bed that I hadn't yet noticed. "You would've had to lift the board off the bottom of the wardrobe to get to it. It's a nice hiding place."

"Bernice," I say, "I promise I didn't go through that wardrobe. I didn't even know how to get it open. Harry and I left the room, but it was to see if we could find any evidence of an intruder."

"It's true," Harry says. "We found evidence too—footprints in the snow by the library doors."

Bernice's eyes turn dark. "The library?"

I nod my head. "I also tripped over one of the dogs and screamed. That's probably what you heard."

Bernice stares at the wall behind me. The small smattering of freckles on her face delicately zigzag around a line that creases between her eyes. The line deepens the longer she thinks about what we've just said.

"Footprints. I wonder…" She trails off before returning her gaze in our direction. "Do you know what's in this box?" She places the box on her lap before removing the lid.

She pulls out several journals, a thick stack of pages held together by a paperclip, and a couple of photographs followed by a few sheets of old newspaper neatly folded. The contents look aged with dry edges and some visible yellow spots. Bernice takes a moment to run her hand over the paperclipped documents.

"This might sound odd, and it might not make much sense, but I have a gut feeling that whoever broke into this house and hurt Madge might have been after this box," says Bernice.

She stares down at the contents, and I can see the fight in her eyes—trying to decide if she can trust us. She picks up the stack of papers first and hands it to me. "This was the first draft of the last manuscript Lois and I wrote together. It was never published."

Although the stack of paper is thick, it doesn't look like quite enough papers to make a whole novel. The words *The Vulture We Know* are written in typewriter font in the center of the page above the small script *by B. Bookerton and L. Wrighter.*

"The pseudonyms Lois and I picked out. We thought we were so smart picking those names."

"L. Wrighter and B. Bookerton?" Harry peeks at the manuscript over my shoulder. "My grandmother loves your books! I remember when I was little, she used to make me watch *The Paths of the Autumn Skies* with her whenever they played it on TV. She said the movie was almost the exact same as the book."

Bernice waves a hand in the air dismissively, but her mouth raises just a tiny bit in the corner. "That book and movie had a bit of a cult following, but I wouldn't call it a classic."

"I can't believe you're B. Bookerton," Harry says. "I remember my grandmother telling me about the day she found out you and L. Wrighter had stopped publishing. She still tells the story every Christmas when she rereads *A Candle by the Ever-Green Tree*, the last book you both wrote. She said she waited years for a new novel to come out and would drive to all the bookstores within a three-hour radius of her house just looking for a new book. Eventually, she came across a small article about you retiring from writing. Whenever I visit her over the holidays, she still makes me look you up on the internet to see if you've come out of retirement."

"That was the hardest part about giving up writing," Bernice says. "Knowing we had disappointed so many of our loyal readers. Lois and I didn't have a choice though. Not after the last accident."

Bernice pauses and holds the newspaper out to us. *Bookerton and Wrighter Cursed* reads the newspaper headline. I squint at the fading first line of the article:

Famous novelists B. Bookerton and L. Wrighter, known for novels as whimsical as they are dark, have recently become entangled...

Before I can finish reading it, Bernice snatches it from my hand.

"We really should burn these things. It would make everyone safer," she says. The tips of her fingers turn pale as they grip the papers.

"What happened?" I ask.

The line between Bernice's eyes deepens, and she stares at a point on the floor before she speaks. "The media said Lois and I were cursed. All these horrible things started happening around us whenever we were working on a new book." Bernice takes a pause, and a slight tremble from her hand shakes the papers before she steadies herself. "Things would go wrong so often that I started to wonder if maybe we were under a sinister spell of some sort. It got to the point where we both felt like we had to stop writing. Neither of us has worked on a manuscript for ten years."

"What kind of things started happening to you?" I ask.

Bernice purses her lips. "The first thing was a freak accident. The postman was delivering a manuscript to our publisher in New York.

We had just completed the first draft of our third book, *Ice in the Way of Time*. While the mailman was on his way into our publisher's building, he slid on a patch of ice right into the street and was hit by a car. He survived, but it was just the first of many incidents.

"The second thing happened when Lois and I got our first movie deal just a year after the postman event. We were on set, and a fire broke out—burning almost the whole studio to the ground. Everyone got out okay, and no one was hurt, but it was millions in damages. I had been really shaken up about it at the time. For months after, anytime my nose got a whiff of the smell of firewood, I would go into shock. Thank goodness that passed.

"There were other things too. Things that seemed more minor. Thefts of small items, people getting stuck in elevators. Once, while writing our seventh book, a whole bunch of us got food poisoning while we were visiting a restaurant in the Alps. All small things, but they always happened when Lois and I were in the middle of writing a book. If we took a short break, even if it was just six months, nothing bad would happen, but then, as soon as we started writing again, anyone near us or associated with the book we were working on was suspect to catastrophe. It got to the point where we had been working on a book about an avalanche, and our editor actually got swept away in an avalanche. He survived—he got caught up in the tail end—but still. What were the chances?"

"Was the avalanche why you stopped writing?" Harry asks.

Bernice shakes her head. "I wish we had stopped writing then, but, no, we were foolish and decided to write that," she points at the manuscript that Harry is holding.

"It was on the set of *The Timelessness of the Blue Flower*. Lois and I had been given our own movie trailer so that we could write between takes. The whole thing felt fabulous," a small, whimsical light appears in Bernice's eyes before it is wiped out by a darkness. "We were in our trailer writing when it happened. You see, the movie had a huge budget. They thought it would be Oscar worthy. The set designer had flown in a chandelier on loan from a French castle—beautiful, thousands of crystals. It was an antique, dating pre-revolution. Something happened when they were adjusting it. I'm not quite sure as I wasn't there, but it ended up falling on two of the background actors on set. A young man and a young woman. It was a real-life *The Phantom of the Opera* moment. It was as if Lois and I had our own phantom following us everywhere, and no one around us was safe. That's when we decided to stop writing. We never published *The Vulture We Know*."

"That's what you and Madge were fighting about before dinner," I say. I think back to the words that had started the tiff between Madge and Bernice at the dinner table. *They weren't the only thing that were smashed.* Madge had spoken the words intending to upset Bernice.

Bernice nods. "Madge and I always had a delicate relationship, and she liked to push my buttons, but I would never hurt her," she says, suddenly realizing that her words weigh heavier now that Madge's dead.

"What happened to the actors who got hurt?" Harry asks.

Bernice wipes at her eyes, slightly smudging her makeup. "Our publishers tried to shield us from what happened. They didn't want us to feel the guilt. Every time I would ask, I would get redirected to another person who would redirect me to another, but I eventually found out one day by eavesdropping outside my editor's door. The conversation was muffled, but I was able to conclude that the girl died shortly after, and the man lived. I never told Lois. I didn't want her to feel the guilt I felt."

Bernice's hands tremble in her lap. They contain a similar smattering of freckles like the ones on her face. She appears so small in the dim light with her eyes downcast and shoulders hunched, so different from the woman I met at the dining table. Is it possible that this woman somehow hurt Madge because of Madge's callous remarks about something that had happened so long ago? Something in my gut tells me no. Bernice couldn't be this upset if she had been the one to get rid of Madge, but then again, I haven't known Bernice longer than a few of hours.

Bernice fiddles with the watch on her wrist. "It's time for everyone to meet up again." She composes her face so that it looks like she was never crying. "Let's not share a word of this to the others." Her deep voice is back to its natural tone, and she leads the way out of the room.

It doesn't take long for us all to gather inside Charlie's room on the third floor. Lois is sitting on the edge of Charlie's bed while Natalie sits curled up in a desk chair wearing a winter coat with scarf and gloves. Charlie's room is much larger than mine. It has a large writing desk in the corner facing a small window that overlooks the woods, and next to the desk stands his bed, a four-poster made of some kind of warm wood with red under hues. Someone has pointed a flashlight at the ceiling to help spread light throughout the room in the same way that Bernice had done in mine. It works much better than the soft glow a couple of candles might offer.

As hoped, Charlie has come around although he's taken on a gray pallor—not a surprise after all he's been through. Lois lets us know that she's already informed Charlie about Madge's death, which hasn't helped his condition.

"I don't remember anything," Charlie rubs his head. "I remember I walked into the kitchen and, next I knew, I was waking up on the floor. Do you think the same person who attacked me murdered Madge?"

"It's a possibility we all have to consider," Bernice says, gripping his hand.

The room is quiet. The hope that Charlie would help solve the case by revealing who hurt him and absolving the rest of us doesn't seem to be coming to fruition.

"Why were you headed towards the kitchen?" Natalie asks. She brushes a strand of hair back from her face, revealing her deep blue eyes. They're bloodshot with small red lines running through the whites like snakes. "Maybe if you could remember why you went into the kitchen, it could trigger some other memories?" Her voice is light and airy, spreading a comfort in the cold room.

Charlie shakes his head. "I just can't remember."

"That's okay, Charlie," Bernice says. "I'm sure something will come to you eventually."

"What do we do now?" Natalie asks. "The grand plan was to see what Charlie said when he woke up, but he doesn't remember anything."

Bernice exchanges a look with me from across the room. The late night has painted dark half-moons across the bottoms of her eyes. I do my best to read her thoughts before speaking. I can tell she doesn't want me or Harry to mention our conversation about the manuscript.

"Harry and I found some footprints that led to and from the doors in the library. We think whoever hurt Charlie and Madge might've been an intruder," I say.

Natalie stands up from her chair. "A thief maybe? Madge could've surprised them while they were searching the house for valuables. Lois, could you give us a list of anything worth of value in the house? We could scout around in the morning once there is some light to see what might be missing."

Lois nods her head. "I can come up with a list by morning," she says mechanically. The night has sent her into some sort of daze.

"It's best that we all get some sleep. This has been very upsetting," Bernice takes the reins while giving her friend's shoulder a pat.

With Bernice's words, everyone except Charlie disperses. Harry, Bernice, and I all head down to the second floor. Bernice goes into the room that Harry and I had heard whispers from earlier in the night. I wonder if she and Lois had been talking about their past—maybe something to do with the unfinished manuscript *The Vulture We Know*. Harry nods his head towards my door, indicating that he wants to talk in my room. We both go inside, and I close the door quietly.

"I know we found those footprints outside that suggests there was an intruder," he says, "but that doesn't mean that we're all safe inside this house."

"I agree. I can't get the story Bernice shared with us out of my head. She said my wardrobe had been opened and pulled apart while you and I were searching downstairs. If an intruder got inside and killed Madge and then stayed to ransack my room while we were both in the library, there would've only been one set of footprints heading towards the house, but you and I both saw a set leaving as well."

"Exactly. Which means the intruder either left the house and then found another way in that we haven't discovered yet, or the outsider is working with someone else in the house."

"In the morning, we'll figure out some next steps," I say. "I think if we keep skulking around at night, we'll draw too much attention to ourselves."

"Sounds like the best idea. For now, make sure you sleep with your door locked. One murder tonight has been enough for me."

He gives my arm a concerned squeeze before he leaves the room, and my cheeks fill with heat. The part of the human brain concerned with murders doesn't seem to have communicated with the part responsible for human attraction. I really need to get a better control on my emotions if I'm going to continue working with Harry on this case.

I lock my door before tidying the room back up. I won't be able to sleep with everything strewn around. As I pick coats off the floor and straighten things up, I step on something sharp. Glancing down and using my phone flashlight (I have just enough battery left for a glimpse of light), I look for the sharp object. Something glitters in the artificial light. I pick it up and cradle it in my hand. It's a small earring, a blue gem with silver backing.

CHAPTER EIGHT

A WINDY MORNING

I am woken by the sunlight streaming through the window and a room so cold that my breath hovers in the air whenever I stick my head out from under the comforter. It's early morning, and the sky is tinted a warm orange. I've slept surprisingly well despite the lack of heat in my bedroom. My brain must've been in overdrive from all the excitement and been in a happy reprieve to get some shut-eye.

The library is the first room I venture towards once I'm out of bed. The memory of the fire from the previous night undoubtable drives me towards the book-filled room. I'm not disappointed by what I find. Harry is alone and in the process of rekindling the fire. After a few pokes, the flames glow strong, munching away at the logs that feed them, giving a great warmth to the room. Harry jumps when he sees me and lets me know that he was up early in the hopes that Natalie would be awake, and they could go check on their cars and call for help, but she has yet to stir.

Harry settles onto the couch and absently strokes Rockey's head in a light circular motion as he flips through one of the books that he has found on the library shelves. It's one of Lois and Bernice's titled *The Day of the Green Leaf.* Painted poison ivy leaves decorate the dusty book sleeve. Harry's forearm reveals light traces of muscles as he holds the book up with his right hand. He suddenly closes the book with a light thump, startling Rockey, and turns in my direction.

"Don't you find Bernice's story rather peculiar?" He asks me.

"What do you mean?"

"Bernice and Lois write gothic novels, and it's almost like their lives were turned into gothics with all these strange happenings going on around them."

"I think sometimes writers can get in their heads. Artsy types have always seemed a little superstitious to me, and writing is one of the finest arts around."

"Aren't you a writer?" He smiles at me.

I smile back. "I am, but I write about birdwatching. Nonfiction is a very different genre."

Harry stops head scratching Rockey only to be pawed at by the curly-haired mutt. "I wish we knew who went through your wardrobe."

His thoughts remind me of what I found before I went to bed. I pull the blue earring out of my pant pocket. "I found this on my floor last night. It's not mine."

Rockey gives the earring a good sniff while Harry holds it in his hand before passing it back to me. He opens his mouth to say something, but Natalie appears, bundled up in a scarf and gloves.

"It's nice and warm in here," she says. She smiles at Harry, showing off her white teeth.

"Harry, I think you and I should try making our way through the wind to check on the cars. There could be a cell signal up there that you missed last night. If we find one, we can call for help," she says.

I can't help but feel a small stirring in my chest over the thought of her and Harry getting to spend time alone. I shove the feeling down as far as I can but not before scolding myself. I barely know Harry—why am I making such a big deal over him spending time with Natalie?

Harry gets off the couch and gives me a complacent wave before the two of them disappear. I check my own phone once I'm alone in the library. It has barely any battery left. The red battery sign is drained to a small sliver. I tried sending a text to Mom when I woke up today, thinking that she could somehow help us despite being so far away, but I didn't have any luck with the message going through. I even thought about sending a text to Mr. Hawking to ask what I should do now that the scene of my article is the scene of a murder, but then, I thought better of it. I wouldn't want to give my editor any reason to pull my first big story. My phone goes black in my hands—it's officially dead.

I get up from my place on the couch and join Rodeo who is curled up on a window seat overlooking the backyard. The footprints that Harry and I found last night are completely gone—covered with a thin crust of shiny snow that the wind has conveniently placed over them. Rodeo stretches his legs out towards me, pushing against my shins as he gives out a sleepy yawn. If only he knew how nice and warm the library was compared to my room, then I bet he wouldn't be so tired. His ears perk up, and he lets out a low growl from deep in his throat as he watches something out the window.

A small white-breasted nuthatch zooms by the window before landing on a nearby tree trunk. Its white breast is puffed up in contrast to the bluey-gray feathers that wrap tightly against the bird's back. With its long beak and tiny coal black eyes, the tiny songbird carries the face of a grumpy snowman. The bird moves to make its way down the tree through characteristic hops—its head facing down the whole time. I should ask Lois if the nuthatch is a frequent visitor. It would make for an interesting note to add to my article.

"I think the library might be my favorite room."

I look back from the window to see Lois dressed in a flowy emerald green sweater that drapes to her mid-thigh along with a white scarf. Her eyes have heavy blue rings around them, a sign that she must've been up through the night thinking of Madge.

"Madge never cared for the library too much. She found it stuffy, but I was a writer, so of course, I love any room filled with books." She sits down on the couch and both Rockey and Rodeo go to greet her. I have so many questions running through my mind that I want to ask her. I think back to what Harry said about Bernice's story and wonder if there's a way to ask Lois about it.

"Bernice told me a little more about how you were writing partners last night," I pick at a string that has come loose on the window seat cushion.

Lois grows a smile across her face. "I'm surprised she told you about it at all. We stopped writing because she thought we were cursed." Lois lets out a laugh. It's a relief to hear some spirit in her after she was so subdued last night. "Now, I can't help wondering if maybe she was right."

"How so?"

Lois folds her hands and rests them on Rodeo who sits next to her. "I hadn't yet told Bernice, but I had recently started working again on the manuscript we had abandoned so many years ago. She was so worried about some curse coming after us, but I just thought, I'm getting older, and I want to write, so I won't let some silly thought stop me." The whites of Lois's eyes turn slightly pinkish. "But now, Madge's dead."

"Oh, it's not your fault, Lois," I reach my hand towards her in a comforting gesture.

Lois stands suddenly and pulls a piece of notebook paper from her pocket. "This is the list of valuables that Natalie asked for last night. I didn't notice anything missing, so I think Madge must have scared our burglar away. If you don't mind, I'm going to grab myself some iced coffee from the fridge."

Before she turns to leave, she stops herself suddenly and looks at me. "You should probably check on your car. With the storm last night and all those branches coming down, who knows what condition it might be in."

"I probably should," I say.

I leave Lois in the library and go to put my coat and boots on before reaching the front foyer. The great oak door acts as a good shield against the wind that beats outside. I wish I had some sort of hat to stuff my hair up into but tucking it under my red coat will have to do for now. I give the oak door a big push, and the wind pulls it out of my hand, slamming it into the side of the house. It takes a bit of muscle, but I manage to shove it back into place before taking off down the front steps.

The footpath leading to the lane is cluttered with little bits of leaves, needles, and twigs sitting atop the crystalized snow. A large turkey vulture sits near the edge of the path picking at its plumage. It gives a start upon seeing me and flaps away into a grove of pine trees where only its tiny red head is visible against the dark bark of the trees. A small songbird comes out of an old woodpecker hole in the tree closest to me at the commotion of the vulture. It's the nuthatch I watched with

Rodeo just moments ago. His black, bead eyes study me for a moment before he pops back into his hole. I take a step towards him when a big gush of wind comes from my left and slaps a large twig into the side of my ear, causing an unbearable sting. I cry out in pain and hold my hand to the side of my head.

The front door opens and Bernice stands on the threshold, her arms wrapped around her. "Emma, what in the world are you doing? It's not safe to be outside in this weather!"

As if to prove her point, a great gale thrusts itself into the grove of trees behind me, and the trees sway and creak.

"Come back inside!"

I meet her at the doorway, and it takes the two of us to wrestle the oak door shut.

"Why were you outside?" she asks.

"Lois suggested I check up on my car. I was on my way there when I got distracted by a bird."

Bernice shakes her head and rubs a maternal hand up my arm. "Lois has had a nasty shock with what happened to Madge. I don't think she's thinking clearly at the moment. You definitely don't need to go to your car right now. Let's get you into the kitchen where it's a bit warmer."

Bernice guides me to the table and lights a wick sticking out from a mason jar full of wax. The scent of pumpkin fills the room. I take a seat with my back facing the door to the room so that I have a nice view of the backyard through the window.

"Your ear!" Bernice says. "What happened?"

"It got caught by a twig when the wind picked up. I think it'll be fine."

"It's bleeding a bit. Let me get you something to clean it."

Bernice rummages around in one of the kitchen drawers until she produces a bottle of antiseptic and an old, but clean, rag. When she dabs my ear with the cloth, a sharp bite snaps at my nerves before it disappears.

"Thanks," I say as she sets the rag down on the table. It has little dots of red and pink on it.

"Where are the others?" Bernice asks as she takes a seat across from me.

"Lois is in the library, and Harry and Natalie went to check on their cars up on the road and search for a cell signal."

"I hope they don't come back all bloodied like you," she says.

Bernice twists a thin, gold ring around her left ring finger. It's plain without any jewels. I know Lois is a widow because she had been married to my Great Uncle Albert, but I hadn't thought to inquire about Bernice or Madge's pasts. I had just assumed they were spinsters.

"You're ring is very delicate," I say.

Bernice stops twisting her ring and peers down at it. "It was my mother's. She and my father weren't well off when they got married. I'm sure you can tell by the ring." She places her hands flat on the table. "I never married. Lois and I were career-oriented women back in the day. We couldn't let distractions disturb our writing. I would date but never anything serious. Lois only met Albert once we had retired from writing."

I knew what Bernice meant. As a writer myself, sometimes I found my work took precedent over my dating interests.

"Do you ever wish you had married?" I ask.

Bernice's mouth twists to one side. "I'm not sure. Sometimes I think it would be nice to have a partner, but then I look at Lois, and I think, she married, and now she's just the same as me—alone again." Bernice pauses. "Sometimes I don't think there's much of a difference between a widow and a spinster."

"What about yourself?" asks Bernice. "Do you have a young man?"

I blush and the rush of blood seems to agitate my ear because it pangs for a moment. "Not at the moment," I say.

Bernice waves a dismissive hand. "No worries there. The books always make it sound better than it is anyway. I would know—I wrote gothic romances for twenty years after all." She lets out a laugh. It's deep like her voice.

"Was it surprising when Albert and Lois got married? You said neither of you were really the marrying type when you were younger."

Bernice is quiet for a moment. "It was surprising. Lois bought the house right before she met him." She takes another pause. "They actually met in a very strange way."

"How so?"

"In a similar fashion to how Harry and Natalie showed up here. There was a horrible snow storm that came in through the area. It completely blanketed the town, and everyone had to hunker down. It was before I lived here, but I had been visiting Lois at the time for the holidays. The three of us, Lois, Madge, and I, were all decorating the dining room when there was a knock on the door. Lois and I went to answer the door and standing in front of us was the most handsome man. He had a thick head of curly hair and a wonderful mustache. He was completely covered in snow. Apparently, he had been driving up on the road and hit a patch of ice, and his car swerved off the road. It didn't hit anything, but the snow was too deep for his tires to navigate out of the spot."

"That's like a meeting from a romance novel," I say.

Bernice shrugs. "What can I say, it's the truth." She gives the ring on her finger a good twist. "Lois, being the kind of woman she is, invited him to stay and ride out the storm. She made up a room for him upstairs, and he spent a whole week here until he could dig out his car. Of course, by then, the two were smitten. They wrote letters to one another and visited often for a few months. Then, very suddenly, Albert retired from his job and asked Lois to marry him. She said yes, naturally. They got married at one of the local churches. It was a small wedding with just Madge and me in attendance. I was the maid of honor. I always thought Madge might've been a bit jealous of that, but what could I do? Lois was my best friend, is my best friend. I couldn't say no to her."

"They only knew each other a few months before getting married?"

"It was fast," says Bernice. "But as you get older, you tend to know what you want, so you need less time to figure things out."

"That's a love story," I say.

"It is," says Bernice.

I didn't know that Lois and Albert had such an intense romance. It must've been really hard for Lois to lose him after not being married for very long. It's no wonder that she invited Bernice to live with her and rented a room out to Charlie.

CHAPTER NINE

THE DISCOVERY

I stare out the kitchen window, wondering if I'll catch another glimpse of the nuthatch, but each time I think I spot its feathery puff of a body on a tree trunk or limb, it turns out to be a piece of snow. The wind outside has picked up too, and the air is filled with swirls of shaken snowflakes. The amount of snow that is left from last night is just enough to give the ground and trees a light brushing, but the hurricane-like gusts prevent the power from coming back on. Natalie's light voice fights its way into my thoughts as I sit at the kitchen table.

She and Harry enter the kitchen. Their faces are both flushed from the cool winter air, and he's smiling at her. The two look like they've enjoyed their winter outing. I know my own face is flushing too but not from the cold.

"You two look cold," says Bernice.

"What happened to your ear?" Harry places a hand near where the twig hit me and looks closer at the skin.

"I went outside, and a twig hit me," I touch my hand to my cheek, conscious of its warmth. "Bernice helped clean it up. It's nothing, really."

"I'm a writer, not a nurse. Usually when I deal with blood, it's only written on paper. I'm happy that the two of you fared better," Bernice wipes down a small section of the table before standing up. "Now, if you'll all excuse me, I'm going to go use the restroom," she says before bustling out of the room.

"What were you doing outside, Emma?" asks Harry.

"I wanted to check on my car, but I ended up following a bird into some trees."

A small smile forms on Harry's face. I'm not sure if he's amused by my story or if he thinks I'm ridiculous.

"It was pretty rough out there. It's good you didn't get seriously hurt," he says.

"We both slipped on the walking path on our way up to the road," Natalie says. "It gave us both a good shock, but it seems rather funny now that I think back on what we must've looked like."

"The fall also ruined my phone," Harry places his cellphone onto the kitchen table. Its screen is completely destroyed, a spiderweb of a thousand pieces.

"I wish I wasn't so scattered brained all the time. If I had just remembered to bring my phone with me when I left my place last night, we might not all be in this situation." Natalie cuts in as she rests one gloved hand on Harry's arm. She brings the other hand up to fidget with a loose strand of hair. She gives it a small twirl around her index finger.

All the talk about cellphones reminds me of the call I had with my mother just before I met Lois the other night. "I completely forgot, but yesterday evening, I took a phone call with my mom out in the lane when I was still in my car. I bet there's still reception near there!"

"That's perfect!" says Natalie. "Do you have your phone with you now?"

"Yes," I say, "but the battery died just this morning. I wish I had thought of it sooner."

"Bernice said Charlie had a cellphone last night. Maybe one of us could ask if we could borrow it?" says Harry.

"I can go and ask him," I say.

"While you do that, I'm going to run upstairs to my room and change into some warmer clothes now that these are all wet from our fall," Natalie says.

"Not a bad idea," Harry says.

The two leave so that I'm alone in the kitchen again. Outside, the wind continues to pound the trees and thrum against the windows. I venture upstairs to go and visit Charlie. He was so friendly towards me last night. I'm sure he would understand me needing to borrow his phone. It's also not the worst idea in the world as it will get my mind off of Harry and Natalie.

I stroll out into the main hall when the door to the dining room swings open. Bernice makes her way outside of the room before gently closing the door with just a click of the handle. She heads towards the staircase when she looks in my direction. Her face turns sullen, and her lips pull down at the edges, drawing lines near her mouth. She studies me for a second, seeming to ponder something.

Her deep eyes make contact with mine before she whispers, "The body is gone."

I let out a panicked gasp, but before I can say much more, Bernice pushes a finger against her lips, and her eyebrows furrow together. She gestures for me to follow her up the stairs until we reach her room. Similar to Charlie's room, it is much larger than mine. The door opens into a modern sitting area with dark gray furniture and a matching rug.

Farther away towards a bay window, a queen bed is made up in deep yellows and bright reds. Bernice shuts the door and hurries over to me.

"Don't tell anyone what I just told you, especially that young man," Bernice grabs my arms in a firm grip. "I wasn't planning on telling anyone what I found, but you caught me coming out of the room, so it's best that I be honest. Someone moved Madge's body and cleaned up the dining room. It looks like nothing even happened in that room, and that young man is probably the most capable person of doing such a thing."

I shake my head at Bernice's words. I was with Harry when Madge was killed in the dining room. I know he wasn't the one to hurt her. "It could be the intruder again. Harry and I found that trail in the snow last night, remember?"

"Emma, think about it. How convenient was it that out of all the many windows and doors in this house, he just happens to find a trail of footprints coming and going from the first one he checks? Almost like he knew exactly where to look."

"I found those with him, and we didn't even know where we were going."

"Don't be so foolish," Bernice takes a step closer. From this angle, I can see her pupils dilating into a black void of memory. "Take some advice from a woman who has lived through a few more experiences than yourself. You seem to have taken to him quite quickly, but you should never trust a man that easily, especially if murder is involved."

Warmth strikes across my cheeks. I hadn't thought that my affections for Harry had been that noticeable. I thought I had been doing a good job of pushing them down every time they floated towards the surface.

Bernice's eyes grow even larger under her black lashes. "I'm not going to let my guard down around him, and I think you would be wise to do the same."

"Thanks for the advice," I say. "I suppose it couldn't hurt to be more careful."

I take a step back from Bernice and move towards the door. As much as I appreciate Bernice looking out for me, I can't fully trust her yet. If there's anyone to be suspicious of, it's Bernice. Last night my room was ransacked, and she was the one sitting on my bed, and now today, I catch her coming out of the dining room when we all agreed we wouldn't go in there. More than anyone else in the house, she keeps appearing in the wrong place at the wrong time.

CHAPTER TEN

A MISPLACED EARRING

I t's later in the morning, and I've spent the last couple of hours talking to Charlie in his room about the various birds that live in and around Lois's house and exchanging random stories. He still has a mild headache from the night before, but otherwise, he's exceptionally chatty. After my conversation with Bernice, I went straight to Charlie's room as planned. Like the rest of us though, Charlie's phone has run out of charge.

Charlie is sipping from a metallic water bottle as he sits propped up with several pillows on his four-poster bed. His bed has a neat, white duvet similar to one that would be found in a hotel room, and he appears warm despite the chill that's been settling in the room since I first came in here. The space is decorated with hanging photographs of beaches and other travel destinations where the sun likes to shine.

"I moved into this house because I'm a writer too, and I loved the idea of living with other writers, especially people like Lois and Bernice."

"Are you a novelist like them?" I ask.

"I'm a food critic. I fly all around the country eating at these fancy restaurants with Michelin stars and Hollywood-type chefs. I wanted my homebase to be an escape from the city though. That's the thing, fancy restaurants are almost always in cities. I lived in Vegas for a while and New York. Finally, I said to myself one day, Charlie, you have to travel to a new restaurant every week—let your home be your hideaway. Before I knew it, I was living here. We're only a short drive from an airport too, which makes my life easier." Charlie's face morphs into a smile.

I can't help but wonder if he feels a bit isolated out here. Going from the hustle and bustle of the city to Lois's eerie estate isn't exactly an easy shift in setting.

"I know what you're thinking," he says, rearranging a pillow behind him. "Aren't I lonely out here all by myself?"

I smile politely. I hadn't realized my face was that easy to read.

"I'm not lonely," Charlie says. "I really enjoy just being by myself. Even when I eat at restaurants for work, I prefer to go by myself. I'm the ultimate lone wolf. Once in a while I get curious and want some company, like right now, but usually, I can't be bothered with other people. I think that's why Madge and I got along so well. She didn't like to be bothered." Charlie's eye stare down at his lap. "I know some of the others had their issues with her, but she really was a thoughtful soul."

Charlie's black eyes drift over to a photograph of a beach with creamy sand, coconut trees, and a wooden dock. I know that Lois and her sister were close, and Bernice and Madge had a testy relationship, but how were Madge and Charlie together? Did they truly get along as Charlie says, or did they try not to bother one another for other reasons?

I take the break in our conversation to ask the question that's been bubbling beneath my tongue since I got to Charlie's room. "Are you sure you can't remember what happened in the kitchen before Madge got hurt?"

"I wish I could."

Charlie turns quiet before he glances towards the door as if to check that it's firmly shut. "There is something I need to tell someone though. And for some reason, my gut is telling me to trust you," he says in a low whisper. "And my gut is always right, that's why I am such a great food critic.

"Lois had money problems. From what I gather, before her husband died, they would just rip through everything the two of them had, which is part of the reason why Madge didn't take to him so well." Charlie glances towards the door again before leaning in close to me. "This house has thin walls, and I have good ears. Lois had borrowed so much money from Madge in recent years that Madge wanted her name added to the deed."

Charlie's words make everything click. Madge didn't like me or anyone related to Albert because of the financial trouble he had brought upon the family. She probably blamed him for all of Lois's money problems, but could Lois have hurt her own sister over something like money and a house deed? It was hard to believe. Lois had seemed so upset at her sister's death. Not only that, but as someone who has sisters myself, I can't imagine murdering them—despite the many times I might have said I would. If anything, I would protect Kiera and Meg with my life, not take theirs.

Charlie stirs in his bed. "Normally, I wouldn't be discussing this kind of thing with you, but seeing as it doesn't look like help is coming anytime soon, I wanted someone to know. I figured you were a safe bet since you didn't even know who Madge was when you showed up yesterday."

I give him a simple nod. "Normally, I wouldn't be trying to play detective either, but right now, it seems like we're stuck here with a murderer."

I bid Charlie goodbye and slip into the hallway. My ear has started to throb a bit, so I grab a lit candle someone has left on a hall table and wander to the powder room on the first floor to splash some cold water on it. Inside, I take a glance at myself in the mirror. I'm a mess. My dark, blonde hair is bunched into curled tangles more so than usual, and my hair is beginning to resemble a bird's nest. Also, my eyes have lines of red running through the whites. I take some more water from the tap and scrub at my face.

I turn the tap off and hear some low whispers coming from outside the door.

"I'm not sure what I'll do," says someone.

"You'll get on. You always do," says another, deeper voice.

"It wasn't supposed to happen this way," answers the other person. "I would've never done it had I known it would lead to such a mess."

"We all make mistakes. You'll just have to move on," replies the deeper voice.

"It wasn't a mistake. I chose to do it. I just didn't realize all that would come with it. That's all."

Footsteps retreat away from the door, and I quietly open it. I see Bernice and Lois escaping towards the kitchen, their backs disappearing as they leave the hall behind. What could they have been talking about? Before I can follow them, the library door opens and Natalie appears.

"Emma, I've been looking for you. I needed to ask you a favor."

"How can I help?"

"I misplaced one of my earrings."

"Is it blue with a silver backing?" I ask, thinking about the one I found in my room last night.

"It's a pearl, the same type as my other earring," she points to one of her ears with a gloved hand. Her ear is delicate and dainty, unlike my swollen one, and contains a dark pearl. I frown with disappointment at the earring that looks nothing like the one left behind in my bedroom.

"I'm sorry. I haven't seen it. Do you remember when you were wearing it last?"

"That's the thing. I remember wearing it last night, but there was so much going on, I didn't realize it was gone until I woke up this morning."

"I hope you find it," I say.

"Me too," she says.

There's an awkward pause between us as Natalie fidgets with the one remaining pearl still in her ear.

Natalie's glassy blue eyes glance in my direction before she clears her throat. "It probably isn't my place to say this, especially considering all the hospitality that Lois has offered me, but something about this house and all the people who live here just seems really off."

"How so?" I ask. I haven't known Lois and the others much longer than Natalie, so I don't understand how she could make such a snap judgement.

"Never mind," Natalie blushes. "I'm just in my head—a bit disturbed by everything. I'm going to grab breakfast in the kitchen. Are you coming?"

I nod and follow her lead.

Chapter Eleven

THE MYSTERIOUS MAN

After a light breakfast of jelly toast (there was no peanut butter) and several attempts to use the phone that led to no avail, everyone agreed to wait out the rest of the morning in the library where the fire is roaring like a delightful little lion. Despite having food in our bellies and a heat source, tension still consumes the air.

Natalie has taken up a spot in an old recliner in a corner of the room. Long scratches are etched into the side of the chair as if a cat had once used it for a scratching post. Natalie is bundled up in a scarf and gloves despite having the seat closest to the fire. She has changed into a fresh pair of clothes since her morning walk with Harry. Her new scarf is decorated with tiny yellow sequins and complements the yellow vest she's thrown over her sweater. I'm sharing the couch with Charlie. We've continued our conversation from earlier in the day—minus the accusations against Lois. He's gone on to tell me about some of his favorite restaurants and some of the places I need to try nearby. So far,

I have a growing list of food I need to take a bite out of that ranges from elk burgers to fig pizza.

Near the couch, Lois and Bernice have taken up the decorative twin chairs that frame the living room. Lois is reading a book of poetry that she grabbed off the shelf. She clears her throat every few pages but otherwise appears completely lost in her reading. Bernice, on the other hand, stares off into space as she gently pets Rodeo on the head. Her eyes waver towards Harry at the window seat every few minutes as if to check on his whereabouts. He's watching the wind rumble up the snow outside along with Rockey. I can't help but study his profile against the window. He has a nice tipped nose that stands out against his sharp jawline and rounded cheeks. I self-consciously pat at my own small chin and chapped lips, pretending to wipe away flyaway hairs but really checking for jelly residue from breakfast. I wouldn't want Harry to think I was a slob.

I've never had the best reputation when it comes to the art of romance. Throughout college, I had one on-and-off boyfriend who my roommates nicknamed Buddy because they felt that he would never be a permanent fixture in their lives, or mine, so there was no point in actually learning his name. We broke up for good shortly after graduation. Since my time at the newspaper, I've probably gone on a handful of failed dates—one of which involved me stepping in a large pile of dog poo and smelling rather lovely.

Harry sees me staring and gives me a weak smile. Unfortunately, Bernice notices too and gives me a look of warning. I fix my eyes on a small pull in the rug nearby the couch so that I can avoid both of their stares.

"Maybe we should get to know each other a little more?" Natalie says. "Emma, what's your story? What brings you here?"

I shift in my seat. I hadn't been expected to be called on so soon. "Lois is my great aunt, and she agreed to let me stay here for a bit so that I could write an expose about *Nuthatch Nest* for the magazine that I work for."

"That's fascinating," says Natalie. "Have you learned anything interesting about the house? I would love to know more about its history."

"Not really." My cheeks color. "I've been a bit distracted."

"What about family? Any live around here other than Lois?" Natalie asks.

"Well, I have two sisters, an older one named Kiera and a younger one named Meg. I see them once in a while, but we're not too close. Other than that, my dad's family is huge. I'm related to Lois on his side."

Bernice sits up straight in her chair, disrupting Rodeo from slumber. "I like this getting to know each other idea." She theatrically looks around the room before settling on Harry. "Let's start with Harry. Tell us about yourself, Harry."

Harry turns toward the group, placing his back to the window. "My last name is Starling. I grew up in the Washington D.C. area so not very far from here."

Bernice smiles in kind. "Tell us something interesting! Don't just read us a resume."

"When I was in high school, I was captain of the varsity baseball team."

Bernice waves her hand dismissively in the air. "No, no. Tell us where you were going last night and how you ended up stranded here. Tell us something interesting," as Bernice talks, the hard "T" sounds seem to take precedent as her patience wanes.

"Last night, I got a late call that I needed to head into work because of an emergency. I had just touched down at the airport because I had been visiting my aunt in Arizona. I decided to take the backroads instead of the interstate because I thought the interstate might be jammed with cars. While I was on my way, my car hit some ice, and I collided with Natalie."

Natalie smiles at the mention of her name. She's sitting on the edge of her chair like a well preened bird. It seems fairly obvious that she is a little more than interested in Harry and his stories. Which, I remind myself, shouldn't matter to me because I'm focusing on a murder investigation and not some man I've just met.

"A work emergency so late in the night," Bernice says. "Where did you say you worked again?"

"I work at a hospital," he says.

My stomach flips. Yesterday he had told me he was an accountant at a detective agency. Why is he telling the group a different answer than he told me? My reaction doesn't go unnoticed by Bernice. I am starting to wonder how much more she knows about Harry than myself and if I've been incredibly foolish for aligning with a stranger.

"What about you, Natalie?" Bernice says.

Natalie brushes aside a strand of hair that's fallen over her eyes. Her face is dewy, and a pleasant color shines across her cheeks. "I was on my way to a friend's house. We were going to have a girls' night. Obviously, that didn't happen."

A large clap rings out through the house, the sound rumbling the walls and shaking the floor. The two dogs go off howling, and Lois stands from her chair.

"That sounded like it came from outside," Bernice says.

"We need to go check," Charlie adds, "together. No one should be left alone."

"In this weather?" Bernice looks displeased.

"I think it's for the best," counters Charlie. "A sound that loud needs to be investigated. We'll just have to be careful."

Bernice reluctantly concedes to Charlie's plan, and the group of us stumble into our thick jackets and heavy boots before heading out the front door towards the lane that goes away from the house. Lois leads the way. There's a mild break in the wind, so I am not concerned about getting hit in the ear by a twig this time. I notice that the section of walkway that Harry and Natalie must've slipped on earlier in the day has been covered with a thin layer of snow from the wind, so it no longer serves as a hazard. It doesn't take us long to go beyond the bend in the road and arrive at my car to discover the source of the sound. The large walnut tree that had lost a limb the previous evening is now uprooted. A tangle of rootstock is upended from the ground, and the tree has toppled onto my car, completely crushing the front window and hood.

"I knew something like this would happen with all these old trees and all this wind," Bernice says.

Harry approaches the car to better survey the damage when he jumps back.

"What?" I ask.

Natalie rushes forward and gasps, pulling away from the car and grabbing Harry's arm in the process. "It's a body."

"Madge?" My mind goes back to what Bernice told me about how Madge's body had been taken from the dining room. Had someone moved it to my car?

"No, it's a man," Natalie says.

"A man? Are you saying there's been another death?" Lois's voice quivers with the cold air around it.

I creep closer to the car and glance inside. Sure enough, a body of a large man is bloodied and dead as it sits in my front seat. He's wearing a burgundy scarf, and his dark hair is slicked back, revealing a light-colored scar slashing across his forehead in contrast with his otherwise plain features.

Chapter Twelve

A Short History of Nuthatch Nest

The six of us are back in the library. The sun is peaking out of the sky in a hazy aura, and the dogs are impatiently pacing in front of the library's French doors, begging to go for a walk that keeps getting delayed by the day's events. Lois has let them out to do their business a couple of times, but she is unwilling to let them go beyond a few steps of the door after everything that's happened.

Harry has taken the spot at the window back up and is playing with his watch. The sun reflects off of its pale face as he twists it around his wrist. I don't trust much of what he says after lying about his job.

One thought keeps repeating in my mind over and over. *How did that man get in my car?* I could've sworn it was locked. I had even gone upstairs to my room and checked for my keys when we all got back inside. Sure enough, they hadn't left my purse pocket.

Rockey paws at the ground near Lois's feet before giving up and collapsing with an impatient pant by the fire while Rodeo stares mournfully out the window at an old walnut tree where a squirrel prances up and down. *The walnut tree by my car.* Of course! I had completely forgotten that Lois had told me to lock my car right before the walnut tree's branch had fallen. I must've been distracted and forgotten to do so.

"Why did you think Madge was in your car?" The fire crackles behind Natalie while she looks at me with a growing curiosity. She is the first one to break the silence in the library.

"I don't know," I say.

Bernice catches my eye, a warning.

"I think because Madge had just died, and I was still thinking about her," I say.

The room goes quiet again with the only sounds being Rockey's renewed scratching at Lois's feet and occasional whine of complaint. Over the fireplace, a collection of framed photos is arranged. The one in the middle is of three young women smiling on a sunny beach. Two of the women look like twins, and the third resembles a young Bernice with her dark hair spread across her shoulders and her dark skin glimmering in the sun. I can't imagine the pain Lois and Bernice must be going through with the loss of Madge after having her by their side for decades. Before I can feel too bad for either of them though, Charlie's words about Lois's debt echo in my mind as do the memories of Bernice's continuous bad timing when it comes to showing up places where she shouldn't be. Lois or Bernice could very easily be the murderer. Sometimes contempt is bred in close quarters.

"Lois, do you have any idea who that man in the car might've been?" Natalie asks.

"I don't have any idea," Lois says. "We're out in the country, and once in a while, we might get a wanderer, but I wouldn't expect anyone to be out in weather like this. Or fiddling with someone else's car. I've never heard of a car thief in the area."

My mind travels back to the shadow in the woods I had seen on my first night at Lois's and the footprints that Harry and I found leading to and away from the library. Is it possible that the man we found in my car was the very intruder who had hurt Madge? And nature had decided to take care of him herself with a fateful fall of an old walnut tree?

"If only we could've seen how he died," Charlie says.

"A tree fell on him," Natalie replies.

"No," says Charlie. "We know a tree fell on his body, but who's to say that he wasn't already dead when he was sitting in the car? Whoever killed Madge could've gotten him too."

"You think there was a second murder?" Bernice asks.

"The car wasn't warm or turned on when we found him. I don't know why he would just be sitting in a cold car," says Charlie. "I know I'm still recovering from the fall I took last night, but I think my heads on straight enough to suggest that he could've been murdered just like Madge."

The warmth of the fire sits in my stomach and sends an ache through my body. Before we found the body in my car, there was always the idea that we all might be safe since an intruder could've attacked Madge and fled, but now that a second killing is on the horizon, that glimpse of safety has evaporated into the stuffy library air. I quietly excuse myself into the hallway. The cold air feels like a hug against my clammy skin, and I rest my head against the wall, letting my thoughts swirl. Lois could have killed her sister because Madge wanted her name on the deed. Bernice could've killed Madge because they didn't get along. And then, there's Harry. He lied to everyone about his job—or he lied to me about his job. I can't keep up with all the changing possibilities. I can only hope that the phone lines and power come back soon.

A hand places itself on my shoulder, and I jump. Harry stands behind me.

"You left the library. Are you okay?"

I look into the brown of his eyes and see a small freckle of yellow in the right one. Despite how open his face appears, I remind myself that he could be the most dangerous person in this house.

"I'm fine. It just got really hot in there."

He gives my arm a squeeze that lets me know that he doesn't believe my explanation. After everything that's happened, and even though I know I shouldn't trust him, the gesture still feels comforting. I pull away so that he has to drop his hand.

"Why did you lie about your job?" I ask.

"I don't trust anyone in this house other than you. It's possible that the murderer could be sitting in that room right now, and they could decide that I'm their next target because I work for a private investigation firm, even just as an accountant. I'm sure you can understand why I would be unwilling to take that risk."

He gives my arm another friendly squeeze, except this one doesn't feel as genuine as the last one. I can't help but feel like he's not telling the whole truth. I cross my arms. Harry is staring back at me with raised eyebrows.

"I think this whole situation is fishy, and I'm not sure who I can trust," I say before walking away.

I don't go back into the library. I've been a guest at Lois's house for one night, and I already feel like I need to escape. I wander down the hallway instead, knowing that I can't disappear. At the end of the hall, there's a large arched entryway that opens up into what I presume to be a study. Unlike the warmth of the library, the study is cold in more ways than one. There's a large desk positioned in front of a barren fireplace and a dusty antique globe standing erect between two leather arm-chairs that look more like stiff, disapproving sentries than comfortable spots to sit. The room faces the forest line, so only dim, shadowy light comes through the windows.

The only spot of bright color comes from a thick, hardcover coffee table book lying on the sideboard nearest the window. I run my fingers over the front of it and recognize the house on the cover immediately. It's *Nuthatch Nest*. The photograph used for the cover must've been taken sometime in the spring because there are blooming blue hy-drangeas and pink azaleas framing the house. The gloomy forest has also transformed into a backdrop full of green life. I flip the book open and glance at the title on the cover page: *Historic Homes of the Eastern United States*. I thumb through the book, looking at pictures of large, notable homes until I come across the same photograph from the cover of the book.

Underneath the large picture is the caption: *Nuthatch Nest*. I turn the page and find more pictures of the home along with a small list of facts and a blurb. The page includes information like the year the home was built, *1878*, the name of the man who built it, *Ralph Swanhild, a millionaire recluse*, and the fact that *Swanhild's wife's favorite bird had been the white-breasted nuthatch*. It's all information that I learned about the house before coming here. One fact catches my eye though. The book states that *Swanhild built the home after the sudden death of his wife*. That was news to me. I would have to remember that for the emotional angle of my article.

"I see you've found the study," Lois leans against the window and gazes out into the woods.

I close the book quickly. "I'm sorry. I didn't mean to snoop. It got a little too warm in the library, so I needed a break."

A small smile sketches itself against Lois's face. "I wouldn't call it snooping to sift through a coffee table book."

"I just wanted to know more about *Nuthatch Nest*. I haven't had the opportunity to sit down with you and discuss the house. I know so little about it."

"I suppose the old house's history was what appealed to me. Being a gothic writer, how could I resist the temptation of an old, stately home with a tragic past?"

"Tragic past?"

"Quite so I'm afraid. Like the book says, Ralph Swanhild built it after the death of his wife, and he named it *Nuthatch Nest* after her favorite bird. A kind man he was, for she did not have the most noble of deaths. Died at the hands of her own sister because it was thought that she, Swanhild's wife, was in love with her brother-in-law, the husband of the offending sister."

"That's awful," I say.

"It is. Ralph built the home to escape everyone. That's part of the reason why it's so secluded."

Lois rubs her hands up and down her arms. "I'm getting a chill just standing in here. I hope you don't mind if I leave to go back to the library. You're free to look around wherever you like, of course. Despite the history of this house, I can assure you it doesn't have any secrets."

She affectionately pats me on the shoulder before departing from the study. I watch her leave. Her posture isn't as poised as the night that I met her. No doubt, her sister's death has affected her in more ways than one.

I'm still holding the coffee table book in my hand, so I put it back down on the sideboard. As I shift it into place, something slides from between its pages and flutters to the floor. I bend to pick it up when I see that it's a contract of sorts. The top is faded, and the paper is thin, the type of thing someone might get from a bank when they receive a carbon copy receipt. I gasp and hastily tuck it back inside one of the pages of the book before my mind can react to what I've just seen.

It appears that Charlie wasn't lying when he said that Lois had money problems. According to the paper, now hidden away in the coffee table book, Madge had loaned Lois fifteen thousand dollars just a few months ago. Why would someone need that type of money? Especially someone as successful as Lois?

I straighten the book on the table, so it looks the same as it did when I first came upon it. There are other interesting trinkets in the study that catch my eye. There's a photograph of Lois's dogs framed on the desk. They look to be just a little bit older than puppies. Rodeo has his paw around Rockey, and the two are looking off in the distance. Behind them, a man is standing with a big smile on his face while holding up a bouquet of flowers. I take this to be my Great Uncle Albert based on the resemblance he has to my own grandfather. The two men possess the same gray, curly hair and long sideburns. Great Uncle Albert is also wearing a silver watch with a pale lavender face. It looks oddly familiar. Maybe my grandfather has a similar one.

I set the frame back down when a burst of wind rattles the house. Outside, a bird nest falls from a tree. The storm seems to be upending everyone's lives.

Chapter Thirteen

THE VULTURE

Charlie has scrounged around the kitchen to find enough ingredients to make us a lunch. He's chopping a large head of lettuce up rhythmically while a bowl of minced carrots sits in front of him. The rest of the kitchen is covered in candles that Lois and Bernice collected around the house.

After the realization in the library that the man in my car might be another victim of murder, no one has attempted to broach the topic, and only polite conversation has been exchanged. Harry sits at the table with Natalie, talking in a low voice that I can't catch. She leans towards him in great interest. After his lie in the library, my cheeks no longer get hot at the idea of her flirting with him. Harry motions for me to join him and Natalie at the table, but I pretend not to see him and choose to ask Charlie about his cooking methods instead. Harry looks upset but turns his attention back to Natalie.

Lois hovers near the sink. She's wearing a pair of earrings that catch on the candlelight. The emerald earrings pegged in her lobes are almost an exact match for the sapphire one I found in my room last night.

"Lois, your earrings are rather pretty," I say.

Lois touches her studs. "They are nice. Madge and I bought matching pairs a few years ago. Hers were blue."

"They're quite stunning," I say in a cool voice, but the earring in my pocket is burning a hole through the fabric of my pants.

The blue earring that I discovered in my room belonged to Madge! While it's possible that the earring has nothing to do with the murder, and it's just an object left behind from long ago, something darker itches at my senses. What if Madge had been in my room just the other night and had been caught by someone who didn't want her there. Who though? And why would they be mad that she was in that room in particular?

Some of the candlelight catches on Charlie's knife and the silver light glints off of the shiny metal. *Silver.* The night I met Madge, the same night she was murdered, she was wearing a silver and blue pendant and matching bracelet. If she had wanted to complete the look, there's no doubt that she would've selected a pair of silver and blue earrings. I need to go search around my room where I found the earring if I'm going to get to the bottom of this murder.

I take a seat at the table near Lois and Bernice as Charlie busies himself by opening what looks to be a homemade jar of some kind of vinaigrette sauce. Even though I ate just a few hours ago, I can't help it when a low rumble comes from my stomach. It's not long before Charlie places large bowls of cold pasta in front of each of us, and the aroma of spicy vinegar fills the air.

"This looks great, Charlie," I say before taking a bite of the dish. "Did you make the sauce from scratch?"

"I wish I did. I have a friend in New York who makes his own Greek vinaigrette with an old recipe passed down to him from his grandmother. He runs a little café in midtown. If you ever visit, I strongly recommend stopping by just to try the homemade pita chips."

"It's fantastic, as usual," says Bernice as she scoops up some noodles. "I'm not sure if you should be doing so much cooking so soon after your accident though."

"I feel perfectly fine. In fact, I think cooking is rather soothing to the soul, so I should be doing it as much as I like."

Across from me, Lois plays with the pasta on her plate by pushing it into the corners. The jewel on her earring glitters momentarily as she turns her head to the side to listen to something Bernice is saying. If Lois can afford emerald jewels and a historic home, it doesn't make sense for her to have to borrow fifteen thousand dollars from her sister. Surely if she ran into money trouble, she could just auction off an old signed manuscript instead of borrowing from Madge. I wish Charlie had known why Lois needed the money so badly. It would certainly clear some things up.

"What did you think, Emma?" asks Bernice.

"I'm sorry," I say. "I was lost in my thoughts for a moment. What was the question?"

"I asked what you thought of the story of *Nuthatch Nest*? Lois told us that she found you reading up on the house in the study."

"What was the story?" asks Harry from the other end of the kitchen table.

"It's a rather sinister one," says Bernice. "The house was built long ago in the 1800s by a man who was heartbroken over the death of his wife. He named it after her favorite bird, the nuthatch."

"That's not sinister at all. I find it sweet," says Natalie.

"Except his wife was murdered by her own sister. Stabbed right in the heart when her sister found a hidden trove of love letters that she had written to the sister's husband."

"Why would he still name the house for his wife after such a betrayal?" asks Natalie.

"I think that's what makes the story beautiful," says Lois. "It's complicated just like human nature."

"Many of the more historical features of the house that date back to its construction include little allusions to Ralph Swanhild's love for her," says Lois. "For example, the shelves in the library that are built into the house, Ralph had them made from lumber he had shipped in from his wife's hometown miles away."

"When Harry and I first came to the house, we saw that the doors had some type of knocker in the shape of a bird. Is that a reference too?" asks Natalie.

"Those are tiny nuthatches. He had two made to represent a mating pair. He obviously was thinking of himself and his deceased wife when he had them installed," says Lois.

I think back to the two silver knockers on the door that I noted when I first arrived at Lois's house.

"If you look on the banister by the stairs, there are also tiny imprints of nuthatches decorated around the rails," says Lois. "All tiny touches Swanhild included just to commemorate his beloved."

"How did you learn so much about the house?" I ask. "When I was researching *Nuthatch Nest*, I couldn't find any detailed information."

"The nearby town has a small historical society that they keep up. They have a whole section on *Nuthatch Nest*. They're a bit old fashioned too, so if you want to learn more, you have to go to the place in person or call them on the phone," says Lois. "When I bought the house, the previous owners also gave me a few rare books about the old place. You probably wouldn't be able to find them on the internet."

"What happened to the sister?" asks Natalie. "The one who murdered the wife? Did she get away?"

"I'm not sure," says Bernice. "One would hope they caught her."

Lois's utensil clatters on her plate.

"I'm so sorry! I had a dizzy spell for a moment. It just came on quickly. I get them when I'm not feeling well." Lois dabs her napkin around her mouth. "I feel fine now. Don't let me distract from the meal."

"Charlie, this is some of the best pasta I've ever had," says Harry from his end of the table, changing the subject.

"I'm telling you. If you're ever in New York City, you must stop by my friend's restaurant," Charlie gets up from the table and begins gathering plates. Most of them are clean with the exception of Lois's which is still full of food.

After lunch, Charlie goes off with Lois to help her find a battery powered emergency radio she swears Albert bought her several years ago for an anniversary gift. It takes some convincing for us to let her go without a rest after her spell, but she insists that her dizziness comes and goes, and it's nothing to worry about.

The rest of us end up in the library. The wind has picked up outside, sweeping most of the remaining snow off the tree limbs and even revealing yellow patches of dead grass on the lawn. Every few moments, a gust punches at the old house with such force that Rockey, who has taken to following Bernice around, scurries under a nearby desk or table and whimpers. Everyone agrees that even though the snow is not preventing us from leaving, the wind would make it too dangerous for us to go for help on foot. We just have to keep waiting out the weather.

Bernice has procured a fading set of playing cards from somewhere in the library, and Harry, Natalie, and I sit on the floor by the coffee table playing War. I am losing quite badly as my mind keeps thinking of what kind of excuse I could make to go explore my room and look for clues about the earring. I need to learn more about where that earring came from if I'm going to help catch Madge's murderer.

Rodeo has his head in my lap, and he's in a deep sleep, oblivious to all the chaos happening around him. While we play, I study my counterparts, trying to gauge information from their appearances alone. I already know that I can't trust Harry despite his friendly smile and the boyish glint in his eyes. Sitting so close to Natalie, I realize I know barely anything about her. She's still wearing her single Tahitian pearl earring from earlier in the day, and every time she plays a card, she brings one of her hands up to twist it in her ear. I also notice that she might be a little bit older than I had originally assumed. I can see light lines between her eyes and just a hint of crows' feet under her heavy makeup.

I finally lose all the cards in my hand before giving myself a big stretch and announcing that I need to go grab a warmer sweater from my room. Rodeo tries to follow me, but he changes his mind when he realizes I'm forsaking the warmth of the library for the coldness of the hallway. I don't run into Charlie or Lois on the way to my room. They must still be hunting for the long-lost radio. It could take some time to find something that's gone missing in a house this size.

My room feels more like an ice fishing tent than a bedroom when I enter it, and it smells like one too. The wind is screaming through the window, making the space incredibly unwelcoming. My eyes fall over the wardrobe which is neatly closed up just how I had left it after cleaning the mess last night. I go over and pull the doors open. Immediately, the distinct smell in the room envelopes me. Sitting on the bottom of the wardrobe is Lois and Bernice's manuscript *The Vulture We Know*. On top of it lies a dark, dead vulture. I take a step closer and let out a breath of relief. The vulture isn't real, it's just an old dog toy with a pungent smell similar to an old fish. But that doesn't matter. What matters is *who* would put something like this in my room?

CHAPTER FOURTEEN

THE FOX HOLE

"We just have to crank the handle a few times, and it should start working," Charlie and Lois have found the emergency radio and brought it into the library.

I haven't spoken a word about the toy vulture I found in my wardrobe, nor have I touched it. As far as I'm concerned, it's probably related to Madge's death, and I'm not stupid enough to get my DNA mixed up with murder evidence, or let the murderer know that I found their little message to me. I have no doubt in my mind that someone in this house is exceptionally dangerous, and I won't let the same fate as Madge and the man in my car befall me.

I squeeze the sides of the old leather notebook that I'm holding in my hands. Lois let me borrow it. After I found the toy vulture, I asked her if she had some pen and papers lying around so that I could jot some notes down. The battery on my laptop had died, and I needed somewhere to write down information for my article. Work is exactly what I need to focus on to get my mind off of the fake vulture in my room.

The radio produces some static before a voice comes through the speakers. "The wind gusts will continue into the early morning hours. The area is under a severe wind warning, and the weather desk is advising everyone to stay indoors and seek shelter immediately. It's estimated that 450,000 people have lost power in the area alone. Emergency vehicles and centers are running at full capacity, with many reporting that their 9-1-1 calls are not getting through." The voice cuts away to be replaced by a commercial for women's swimwear, so Charlie shuts the radio off.

"I never thought I'd be stuck somewhere because of a windstorm. Let alone after a murder," says Charlie.

A gust of wind shakes the house after the word murder. The natural world seems to be just as displeased with the situation as Charlie. I focus my gaze out the bay window of the library. The nuthatch makes an appearance despite all the wind. He bobs slowly down a large beech tree like a fishing lure in a frothy sea. His chest is puffed out, something songbirds do when it's cold outside.

"Madge always enjoyed birdwatching," Lois says as her eyes follow mine to the white-breasted nuthatch. "I had been hoping that you and her might be able to bond over that," her voice trails away.

"Wasn't your last manuscript about a bird? A vulture?" I ask.

Lois sits up from the chair she's been occupying. "Yes, it was going to be called *The Vulture We Know*. How in the world did you know about that?"

Bernice's eyes dart towards mine as the dark of her irises melds into her pupils. "I might've mentioned it to Emma in passing when we were discussing writing."

Lois has paled. It was only just this morning that Lois informed me that she had started writing the unfinished draft again. There must be multiple typewritten copies of the manuscript for her to be working on it since the one Bernice had shown me and Harry last night is currently in my room.

"What's it about?" Harry asks.

"It is about people who try to take things that don't belong to them. A gothic of course. We set it in the English countryside in the moors in a house not unlike this one. It hasn't been touched in years though, so there's no point in talking about what could've been." Bernice says.

"Spooky," says Natalie.

"I've seen vultures around here before. Usually, when I'm driving out on the roads, I might see one or two," says Charlie.

"Probably those turkey vultures," Lois replies. "We used to have one that would sit on the roof of the house although I haven't seen it in some time."

Someone in this very room is feigning innocence as we speak about vultures. Someone in this very room put that dog toy in the wardrobe to give me a scare.

I doodle on the notebook that sits in my lap as the others start to talk about some TV show that I've never seen. I draw in circles, never ending spirals up and down the page. So many strange things have happened, and I've been at *Nuthatch Nest* for less than 24 hours. Surely, they all must be connected somehow. The man in my car, Charlie's accident, and Madge's death followed by her missing body—why would someone do all those things? Not to mention the preoccupation someone seems to have with the manuscript upstairs.

I think back to Madge's death. Harry and I had been sitting in the kitchen together when we heard the thud. Was it possible that she knew who her attacker was, and that was why we never heard a scream for help? If a random intruder had appeared in the dining room, she undoubtedly would've screamed. And, if one of the five people breathing in the warm fireside air in this very room with me had killed Madge, why had there been footprints leading to and away from the house then? And lastly, why move her body? Six people had seen her dead, disposing of the body wouldn't deny a murder.

I wish I could go outside and have one more look at the man in the car. I can't help but think that he enshrouds some important clues. A gust of wind pushes against the house and the library windows shiver in response. Natalie moves a little closer to the fire, her scarf an anaconda wrapped tightly around the top of her turtleneck.

Eventually, Lois scraps together a delicate charcutier board for a midafternoon snack. There's a variety of thin sliced sausage and thick cut cheese arranged artfully on the board with a side of crackers. I grab some soft cheese and spread it on a cracker. Lois pours everyone glasses of effervescent cider, the kind that family's drink on New Year's Eve without any alcohol. Considering the circumstances, I can't imagine drinking anything heavier would be a good idea.

"I guess that's one nice thing about losing power when it's cold out," Charlie says. "The whole house turns into a refrigerator, so you don't have to worry about food going bad."

Bernice makes up a cracker for herself before speaking. "This whole thing eerily reminds me of a trip that Lois and I took when we were younger."

"Which trip?" asks Lois.

"The trip to that tiny town in the Appalachian Mountains. Remember, we rented a cabin so that we could write, but also so we could learn more about the setting of the book we were working on, *In the Mountains the Clouds Cry.*"

"I remember that book," Harry says. "It's one of my grandmother's favorites."

"It was a bestseller for a while," says Bernice.

"I think I've seen the movie based on that. It was so romantic," Natalie says, sitting on the edge of her seat. "I'll never forget that kiss in the mist between the General and Ms. Cathaway while they stand on a fallen tree alone in the forest."

Lois smiles. "That was a lovely scene to write."

"Except I wrote it," Bernice says.

Lois's pale cheeks blush pink. "Of course, I remember that now. I still loved reading it though."

"Lois always wrote the darker parts of our novels. The castles or the abandoned houses and the sounds that go thump in the night. I usually did the romantic aspects." Bernice says. "It seems that the best gothics tend to have both."

"Why does what happened here remind you of that trip?" I ask Bernice.

"There was no power in the rustic little cabin," Bernice's eyes seem to focus on some point in the distance. "It was so cold, and we had to keep the fire roaring all night. I'll never forget Madge had come with us. She had really taken to the setting and the nature, especially this little fox and her kits. They must've had a home nearby because every evening, she would bring them out for a play right by the front porch. Then, about a week into our stay, Madge had gone out for a walk, and she found the whole fox den had been destroyed."

"A bear or another animal after some food most likely," says Harry.

Bernice shakes her head. "No, we think a human did it because there were footprints deep in the mud around the edges of the den. Someone had just filled in the hole and stomped on all the foliage in the area. It was such a peculiar thing to do. Of course, we didn't see the foxes after that. Obviously, the mother moved homes now that her den wasn't safe."

"It sounds like the curse," I say.

Bernice nods her head. "No doubt."

"What curse?" asks Natalie.

Lois shifts in her seat and rearranges her hands. "Years ago, whenever Bernice and I were working on our manuscripts, unfortune events seemed to befall us everywhere we went. A silly idea, really."

Lois's eyes move towards the fire so that she can avoid looking at anyone. Her tone is different from earlier when we were alone in the library, and she had been lamenting the curse, wondering if the death of her sister was somehow her fault for writing again.

"It's all much too dark to talk about," says Bernice. "I apologize for bringing it up. I don't know what I was thinking."

The room returns to its silence with the exception of Charlie who is making himself a mini cheese and sausage sandwich from the charcuterie board.

"Emma, why don't you and I grab some more firewood? Lois says she has a bundle in the cellar, and the stairs are just down the hall," Harry suggests from his seat on the couch.

I hadn't noticed, but the fire is indeed dying down to orange embers and a small flame. It wouldn't do to let it go out completely in this weather.

"Sure," I say.

I follow Harry out of the library, silently reminding myself that he can't be trusted and promising myself that I won't turn my back to him. As soon as we are through the door though, Harry turns around and grabs me by the shoulders. His hands alone channel a warmth under my skin that I want to cave into.

"I know you don't trust me after I lied about my job, but I know you've found out more information. You and I have to stick together." He pauses to take one of his hands off of my shoulders so that he can run it through his hair. "We were both with each other when Madge was killed, so we're the only two people clear of the crime."

I look into his eyes, a light shade of brown with a hint of an orange warmth behind them. I bite down on my lip. I want to trust him, I want to trust someone, but Bernice's words won't leave my mind. "How do I know you weren't working with an intruder?"

"Why would I go and look for proof of an intruder and show it to you if I was working with one? Wouldn't I have wanted to keep that a secret?"

He has a point. If he had been intending to get away with his crime, there would be no reason for him to reveal secrets of it to me. Bernice had been firm in her warning though. If anyone in the house had moved Madge's body, it most likely would've been Harry. I close my eyes for a moment and pray that I won't regret what I'm about to do.

"Okay," I say. "I'll work with you. But, no more lies about anything. If I catch you in a lie again, our little alliance, or whatever you want to call it, is done."

"Going forward, I'll be better. No more lies." He smiles, and I note the smoky firewood scent coming off of his fleece.

"Right," I say quickly, reminding myself that trusting him is something I've decided on a whim and not something that I should indulge in too much.

"I found something that I want to share with you," he says.

He pulls out an old photograph and hands it over to me. It has a fold down the middle, but otherwise it is in fairly good condition. In the photo, two women, one blonde and pale and one with dark hair and a splash of freckles, smile brightly at the camera with their arms around a young man wearing dark spectacles who is holding up a copy of *The Timelessness of the Blue Flower*. It takes me a moment to realize what I'm staring at, or rather, who.

"Is that Charlie?" I ask.

"Yes. This morning I found his appointment book left out in the library, and when I got up to glance at it, this slipped out onto the floor."

"He's known Lois and Bernice way longer than he's let on. Why would he lie?"

"I don't think he lied," Harry's fingers dance close to mine as he takes the picture from me. "I don't think he knew Lois and Bernice, but he was obviously a big fan before he moved here."

"That makes sense. Earlier when I talked to him, he did mention that he knew they were writers before he moved in."

"That's not the concerning part though."

Harry points to a woman in the background. She sports the same blonde hairstyle as Lois in the picture, but instead of the blue dress Lois's wears, she wears a green ensemble. It's impossible to see her face though as someone has scratched over it with permanent marker.

"Did he scratch out Madge's face?" I ask.

"It looks like Charlie might have some hidden feelings about Madge." Harry carefully refolds the photograph and places it back in his jeans' pocket. "And not good feelings."

"I should tell you, I found out a few things this morning myself that I haven't shared." I go on to tell him that the earring found by the wardrobe had belonged to Madge and that there's currently a toy vulture in my bedroom that was intended to scare me.

"That can't be a coincidence," he says. "A vulture designed to look dead on a discarded manuscript titled *The Vulture We Know*."

"There's more," I say and tell him about how Lois had started writing the manuscript again—giving fuel to the fire of the idea of a curse.

Harry opens his mouth to reply, but before he can, shouting comes from the library. We both rush inside to see what's going on. Lois is standing near the fire, a hand over her mouth. Charlie is behind her, rubbing her shoulders gently as Natalie prods the fire with a metal poker. Bernice is the one out of place though. Her eyes have taken on the same darkness I saw the night before when she told me about her suspicions towards Harry.

"How could you?" her question is directed at Lois. Her deep and toned voice makes the words all the more powerful.

"Bernice," Lois says quietly while patting at a charcoal-colored spot on her white scarf. "I can't live my life trying to avoid some silly curse."

"You promised!" Bernice says before storming out of the room.

"Somehow that leather journal you borrowed ended up in the fire," Lois says to me. "I bent down to see if I could grab it, and the tip of my scarf caught the flames. Natalie helped put it out. That was when I made the unfortunate mistake of mentioning the curse and of telling Bernice that I had been writing again. Now she's blamed everything that has happened on me."

"This is no one's fault," says Charlie. "The dogs might've been play-ing with the journal when it somehow ended up in the fire. They wouldn't have known it wasn't a toy," Charlie gives Lois's back a friendly pat.

Lois frowns. "Both Rockey and Rodeo know to never get too close to the fire." Lois's cheeks are flushed red. It's the most color I've seen her take on since Madge's death. "I better make sure Bernice is okay." She leaves the room.

"I'm afraid whatever you were writing in there is lost," Charlie says to me.

"I hadn't written anything in there anyway," I say.

"I think I'll take a rest," Natalie says.

I take a seat on the old couch, and both Rockey and Rodeo snuggle up to me. I scratch Rodeo on the head and Rockey behind the ear. The two of them look up at me with glazed, brown eyes and lolling pink tongues.

Chapter Fifteen

HESTER

"I better get that firewood," Harry says. "I wouldn't want it to get any colder than it is now. I can barely feel my toes!"

With all the commotion, I had forgotten that restocking wood had been our original intent upon leaving the room. Since the journal has been added to the kindling, the fire is burning a bit brighter but not enough if we want it to last until evening.

"I'll go with you," says Charlie. "I think I need to get out of the library for a bit."

Harry and Charlie disappear from the room, leaving me alone with Rodeo and Rockey who have decided to be more interested in a rowdy group of squirrels outside than me. The two mutts bob their heads in unison as one particularly fat, gray squirrel jumps from tree limb to tree limb with a bulbous walnut in his mouth. The dogs are sitting poised on the window seat completely enthralled by the show with Rodeo leaning his body against Rockey and Rockey's front paws resting on what looks to be a green book from the library. The novel looks achingly familiar, and I recognize it as the one that Harry had been reading earlier in the day.

The scene gives me an idea. I plop down next to Rockey and remove the book from under his paws. He takes little notice of me as he is still entranced by the squirrel, who is now being chased by another squirrel who wants the walnut. The library is filled with books, and Rockey and Rodeo spend all day in the library without damaging any of the books that are lying around. Why would they suddenly take an interest in the journal that Lois had lent to me when they've never paid a thought to any other book before?

The fireplace has a nice set of kindling tools in a stand next to it. There's a poker and a nice set of tongs along with a few other tools that are unfamiliar to me. I need to be fast if I don't want Harry and Charlie to know what I'm about to do.

Leaving the mutts comfortably entertained by the window, I go for the fire tongs and plunge them into the heat of the ebbing flames, aiming for the journal. I manage to pull the burning book from the fire and toss it onto the tiled hearth before giving it a good stomp to smother any remaining embers. Smoke loops in the air making a curled ribbon of gray. Someone has conveniently left their winter gloves on the coffee table, so I pull one on before grabbing the book.

"Let's see if Rockey and Rodeo are actually interested in you," I say while looking at the journal.

Once the journal isn't completely smoking, I bring it towards the dogs. Thankfully, the squirrels have retired to their nests high up in the trees, so there's nothing that could distract the dogs for my little experiment. I bring the journal over to the two, and they both take a gander. They each give it a benevolent sniff before pattering back to the window.

"It looks like you two aren't very interested in this journal," I say to them.

Rockey passively wags his tail at me, and Rodeo perks his ears up innocently.

I flip through the book, but it is empty. The only writing in it is from me drawing doodles. The book appears to be a dead end. All I've learned from my experiment is that Rockey and Rodeo were definitely not interested in the journal like Charlie suggested. That leaves four people in the library at the time the journal was placed into the flames: Charlie, Lois, Bernice, and Natalie. Lois was the one who tried to grab it out of the fire, so it wouldn't make sense for her to risk burning herself after throwing it in, and Bernice seemed shaken up about the idea of the curse resurrecting itself so that throws a shadow of innocence onto her. That leaves Natalie and Charlie as possible culprits. Another question is left unanswered though that's bothering me more than who tossed the book near the fire. Why would someone put it in the fire? There isn't even anything written in the journal.

I sink my teeth deep into my lip. The journal was a perfect diversion, but for what purpose? What would someone want to do in the library without others looking? I glance around the room and look for anything out of the ordinary or missing. A small table sits by the armchair nearest the fire with a stack of detective novels and gothics resting atop of it along with a bowl of stale looking dinner mints. I concoct the image of someone creating the distraction to hide a book in their jacket, but that seems rather pointless as people tend to take books to and from libraries without suspicion.

I stare deep into the dying fire. The orange and yellow flames bore into the few remaining logs left. If everyone in the room was looking down into the fireplace because they noticed the journal was burning, where were they not looking? Wasn't it possible that someone put the journal in the fireplace as a distraction?

I raise my eyes and focus on the picture of Lois, Madge, and Bernice at the beach. Next to that is what looks to be a wedding photo of who I assume to be my Great Uncle Albert with Lois. She wears a long veil over her face, and Madge traipses in front of her holding a bouquet of sagging lilies. Next to that photo is one of Bernice on a porch with a big smile while wearing an oversized sunhat that covers almost her whole face. I lower my eyes back to the fire below the mantel. Could it have been possible for someone to slip a small frame off of the mantel while everyone else was distracted by the fire?

I go to the mantel and run my index finger along the one side, a thick layer of dust piles onto the tip of my finger to make a grayish finger print. I brush the dust off and swipe the mantel again, but this time from the other side, and I stop. There's a small rectangular section empty of dust near the end of the mantel.

I smile over at Rodeo who has moved and is now wound into a tight circle in his dog bed. I'm not sure if dogs have eyebrows, but I could swear that he has raised his at me as if to congratulate me on my findings. The journal was put in the fire so that someone could remove a photo from the mantel. If the photo frame was small enough, a person could have easily tucked the frame into a jacket pocket as everyone's attention focused on the fire below.

"We're back with the firewood," Charlie bursts into the library. "We had to go to the cellar to get it, and it was freezing. You wouldn't believe the sound of the wind down there!"

Charlie and Harry both settle a bundle of firewood onto the tiles by the fire. I notice Charlie is wearing a tan jacket that has large pockets. It's possible he was the one who sought out the picture and disposed of it when he and Harry went to the cellar. How would I prove it though?

"You've dug out your journal from the flames! How brave of you," Charlie gestures to the scarred journal I left on the coffee table.

"I figured it wasn't good to be burning it in the fire. Who knows what material the cover is composed of?"

"Good thinking," he says.

"Do you mind if I turn the radio back on?" Harry asks as he fiddles with one of the dials. "I wouldn't mind hearing an update on the windstorm."

"Go for it," says Charlie.

The radio comes on with the sound of the broadcaster's deep voice taking command of the library, "The windstorm is predicted to continue on into the early hours of tomorrow morning before it calms down. Work crews are having difficulty restoring power and phone lines across the area as the storm continues to make it tough to work outside. People in need of emergency assistance may have to seek help on foot, but even then, emergency services warn people of flying debris and downed wires..."

"So essentially there is no update," says Harry.

He seems clammy, frustrated almost. His cheeks have a prominent red streak through them, and his brows are creased. "I think if the storm doesn't calm down soon, one of us is going to have to take a risk and go for help on foot."

"On foot?" asks Charlie. "You heard the newscaster. He said it could be dangerous. Also, while this is an awful situation we're in right now, there's really nothing emergency services can do to help us."

"What do you mean?" I ask.

"Madge and that man in your car are dead. There's no sense in sending for an ambulance for them now."

"I'm tired of us not taking action," Harry replies. "There's still a dead body in the house, and it can't just sit there another day."

While Charlie has a good point, it is a bit odd for him to be against seeking help. There has been a murder in the house after all. Is it possible that he's trying to buy time so that he can make Madge's body disappear for good? An image flashes through my mind of Bernice sneaking out of the dining room only to reveal to me that the body has been removed and the room completely cleaned up. That was one piece of information that I had neglected to tell Harry, so he must be unaware that Madge's body has disappeared. Bernice suggested that Harry was the most capable person of moving the body, but wasn't it possible that Charlie had faked his attack in the kitchen and he himself cleaned up the crime scene?

"Let's say we do end up in a situation where one of us has to go for help, who do you suggest goes?" asks Charlie.

"Me of course," says Harry.

"But why you?" asks Charlie. "Why not me? I know the area better. Or Emma? She writes for a nature magazine, so she could probably survive out in the wild the longest of all of us if she got lost."

"I write for a birdwatching magazine, so I probably wouldn't fair that well if I got lost."

"That's beside the point," Charlie says. "Harry, why would you be the one to leave the house?"

Harry shrugs. "I just figured no one else would want to go because of the risk of the storm, but if multiple people wanted to go, we could flip a coin or something."

Charlie grows silent and picks at one of his fingernails. He is obviously suspicious of Harry wanting to leave the house and leave the rest of us here. I wonder if Bernice said something to him or if the two of them are working together similarly to how Harry and I are. Outside, the wind keeps up its rattles as it pushes against *Nuthatch Nest* and all the nimble trees in the forest. A small peak of warm orange pokes out from the sky, and I realize that the sun has started to make its way towards the horizon for the night. Before we know it, we will all be flushed into the darkness again.

Natalie returns from upstairs holding a small, brown book and plops down on the sofa. "Bernice is pretty upset, but she let me take this. She said she forgot that she had it. Apparently, the last time she visited the historical society, she borrowed some out-of-print book about Ralph Swanhild. I'm curious if it talks about *Nuthatch Nest*."

"Have you been to the historical society, Charlie?" I ask.

Charlie shakes his head. "Food is my passion, not so much history. I heard the story about Ralph Swanhild at the same time you did. All I knew was that this house was old and that it was rare. Like a good wine."

"Look at this!" says Natalie. "There's a whole chapter on his wife. Her name was Hester. She was the eldest of two daughters born to a professor of ornithology and his homemaker wife. Her youngest sister, Merle, married a wealthy publisher before Hester married Ralph Swanhild."

"Is there anything else about the murder?" asks Harry.

"It says here that *Hester died under mysterious circumstances not long after her marriage to the much older Ralph Swanhild. Merle became a suspect after it was discovered that Hester had been in love with Merle's husband for years. Hester had been writing him love letters in secret.*" Natalie turns the page. "*But it wasn't a love affair. She never sent any of the letters as they were found to be in her possession at the time of her murder.*"

"She must've gone through her sister's things and found the letters," says Charlie.

"I can't imagine killing one of my sisters," I say.

"Especially considering that Hester never even sent the letters," says Harry.

"Listen to this!" Natalie sits upright. *"After Hester's death, Ralph was inconsolable and decided to retire to the countryside. He built a large house called Nuthatch Nest. On completion of the house, Ralph paid over eight hundred dollars, a large sum at the time, to have the dining room table that Hester's parents gifted them on their wedding day transported to the house. While many might view this as a romantic gesture, the dining room table was where Hester's body had been discovered slumped over after her murder. The large table, estimated to be worth thousands of dollars, still resides in Nuthatch Nest's dining room to this day."*

"The table in the dining room? Why would he want to bring that table here?" I ask.

"He sounds like he went a bit loopy in the end," says Charlie. "Poor man. Overwhelmed by everything that happened."

"It's more than that though," says Natalie. "It's almost like someone purposely killed Madge next to that dining room table. It's like they wanted to recreate the original story."

Harry nods his head thoughtfully. "If someone killed Madge next to the table on purpose, that means they must've known about the story of Hester Swanhild."

The library is silent as the three of us think about the two people who would've known the story of Hester Swanhild. Was it possible that Madge had been in love with Albert, and Lois had killed her for it? That wouldn't make much sense though seeing as Madge wasn't a fan of Albert in the first place. At least that's the impression she had given off. I suppose if Lois was a suspect because of the story, then so was Bernice. Had Madge chased away a man Bernice had once pined for? I doubted it. When Bernice and I had talked in the kitchen, she hadn't mentioned anything about a lost lover or someone she felt that she should've married.

"I don't know," I say. "Lois bought this house a while ago. If she bought it because she wanted to murder Madge in the dining room, she would've done it way before now."

"And if Bernice wanted to murder someone, she would do something original," says Charlie. "She wouldn't go for the sequel."

"You two think it's all a coincidence?" asks Natalie.

Charlie shrugs his shoulders. "I don't know what to think anymore."

Natalie puts the book on the coffee table. "You're right. I'm reading into things and getting into my head. It's just an old story. It might not even be true."

Harry glances down at his watch. "It's about dinner time anyway. Should we try and get Lois and Bernice back downstairs?"

"That's probably for the best," says Charlie.

Natalie picks the book back off of the table and tucks it under her arm. "Do you mind if I keep this for some more light reading?" she asks me. "I know you're trying to write that article and all, but reading helps me take my mind off of things. Maybe I can even find out more information that will help us all get to the bottom of what happened to Madge."

"Of course," I say. "I'm sure there's lots of other stuff I can learn about the house without the book."

"Thanks," Natalie smiles at me and gives my arm a light squeeze.

CHAPTER SIXTEEN

THE FOOD CRITIC

I volunteer to put together a simple dinner for everyone to eat in the library. I'm not much of a cook, but I manage to pull together a tray of cold cut sandwiches from the stock in Lois's refrigerator along with some small bowls of strawberries and blueberries for dessert. I spoon a tiny bit of sugar over the berries before I set the bowls on the tray so that the fruit will create a sweet syrup. It's an old trick I learned from my grandmother.

It takes some coaxing, but Charlie manages to get Lois and Bernice to come to the library for dinner with the rest of the household. After getting some food into their systems, the two women seem to be on much more cordial terms with each other. They even exchange passing remarks on the weather. While people make small talk, I take a deep interest in everyone's attire, trying to determine if they could've discretely hidden a photo frame in their outfit, but this proves a difficult endeavor as I can't quite remember what everyone was wearing at the time of the journal incident. Bernice has draped herself in a cream cardigan that falls to her waist, and Lois has changed into a bulky green sweater, neither of which have large pockets, but both women could've changed outfits from this afternoon. Charlie is wearing a wooly gray pullover without pockets, but I already know that he could've placed the picture frame in the tan coat that he was wearing earlier. Natalie is the only one I know for sure hasn't changed. She's still completely huddled up in her winter coat along with gloves and a scarf.

"Emma, I have to say, as a food critique, you put together a very delectable spread for someone dealing with a power outage. Don't think I didn't notice the choice of Dejon mustard on my sandwich," Charlie says while he gives Rockey a nibble off of his plate.

I laugh at Charlie's remark, fully aware that it comes from a place of politeness and not from a satisfied stomach. "Thanks, Charlie. There were two mustards to choose from, so it was quite a challenge for me in the kitchen."

Harry's mouth twitches at the side as he covers a laugh. "I also enjoyed the dinner. Thanks," he says.

"I definitely enjoyed it," says Bernice while patting at her mouth with a napkin. "I can't believe how quickly it has turned dark. Hopefully it was light enough to get some good birdwatching in so that you can include it in your article, Emma."

"I did see a nuthatch a few times. I'm hoping to catch a better look tomorrow."

"That reminds me," Charlie says. "I have a friend who's also a food critic, and he just did an expose of this restaurant run by a couple of retired ornithologists over in West Virginia. The dining room is situated inside a huge aviary. How they prevent all the birds from stealing your food, or goodness forbid, pooping on it, I don't know, but I just have to show the article to you. It's in a magazine somewhere in my room."

"I'd love to help you look for it," I say.

"I wouldn't mind a walk myself," says Harry.

"Why don't you three go and find it and bring it back to the library while the rest of us clean up?" Bernice gathers plates scattered around the room.

Harry, Charlie, and I all venture out of the library into the hall. Harry has the foresight to bring a sturdy flashlight as there's little natural light left for the day to give. The flashlight illuminates bits and pieces of the stairway as we make our way to the upper floors of the house. Similar to the hallway by the library, the stairwell walls are covered in floral wallpaper, but this paper is yellow with faint prints of buttercups sketched lightly against some kind of maple leaf.

Charlie guides us to his room on the third floor. It looks the same as it did when we were last in here with the exception of his fourposter bed being made up with all its edges tucked in. The desk by the window is stacked with books and papers, and the rest of the furnishings appear undisturbed. Even the curtains that hang gently over the window are still set to the same spot, revealing only a sliver of the outside world.

Charlie makes his way over to his fourposter bed and kneels down. "When friends send me magazines and books, I usually store them under my bed in a plastic bin once I've read them because I don't have the best storage options in this room. I just can't bring myself to throw them away. I'm guessing that's where it is." Charlie pulls out a container one could probably buy at any bulk store. "He did mail the magazine to me recently though, so it really could be anywhere in the room."

"Harry and I will check the desk," I say.

"The magazine has a blue cover and is titled *Eating: Anywhere and Everywhere*," Charlie says with his hands deep in the bin.

On Charlie's desk, he has a thick pile of food magazines. Titles pop out at me in multiple languages along with delicious looking cover images of homemade pies and freshly roasted chickens. I set aside one particular magazine titled *The Great American Cheese and Nut Journal* when something catches my eye in the pile that's not a magazine. It's a small picture frame, just small enough to fit in a coat pocket! Before I can sneak the picture into my own pocket to investigate later, Harry has picked it up.

"This is an interesting picture," he says, holding it out to Charlie.

I stare at Harry's back. I hadn't had time to tell him about the missing picture frame from the library, so he has no idea that he's completely spoiled a possible clue. Charlie gets up off the floor and glances at the picture. His eyes immediately divert to the ground, and a sheen of sweat appears on his forehead like strands of gossamer on dewy morning grass. I peer over Harry's shoulder to get a better look at the photo. It's a colorful shot of Lois and Madge standing in front of a log cabin surrounded by rich green coniferous trees. Beyond the cabin and the trees, the sky has wispy clouds that seem to be about to descend completely into the world below.

"This looks like it was taken on the set of the movie *In the Mountains the Clouds Cry*. That cabin looks too familiar to forget," Harry says.

"That could be," Charlie says.

"Why is it up here though?" Harry asks.

"I think I might know why," I say. I take the picture from Harry's hands and twist the back open so that I can pull the photograph away from the frame. Sure enough, the picture has been neatly folded to focus on Lois and Madge in front of the cabin and obscure the other members in the background—one of which includes a very familiar looking Charlie sitting at a picnic table.

I hand the full, unfolded photo to Harry for him to study.

"I can explain," Charlie says.

"We're listening," says Harry.

"I had to take this picture from the mantel downstairs because I couldn't have someone discovering that I used to work with Lois and Bernice."

"You used to work with them?" I ask.

Charlie nods. "I did, but they don't know. Before I got into food writing, I worked for a company that catered on movie sets. I did a couple with Bernice and Lois. I'm sure they don't even recognize me from back then. I worked in the background. I just worried that if someone discovered the picture and made the connection, they would think I was some stalker who went after Madge, so I hid the picture up here."

"And threw the journal Lois let me borrow into the fire to create a distraction so that you could grab the picture without anyone noticing?" I ask.

Charlie nods. "I wasn't being malicious. I checked the journal and made sure there wasn't any important notes in it before I slipped it in the fireplace. I'm sorry."

"That doesn't explain this picture though," Harry pulls out the photo he showed me earlier with Madge's face crossed out. "This fell out of your appointment book."

Charlie stares at the picture for a second before taking a deep breath. "It's true that I had been fans of Bernice and Lois before I moved in here and had met them at a book signing, but they knew that. I told them that when I interviewed to rent the room. The only thing I didn't tell them about was working on the movie sets. I had heard rumors about the curse when I worked on set, so I thought it best not to bring it up. I didn't want Lois to think that I was somehow cursed and not rent me the room."

"That still doesn't explain why you crossed out Madge's face in the background," Harry says.

Charlie furls his eyebrows. "I didn't cross out Madge's face. She's right there in the picture with me," Charlie points to the vivacious blonde standing next to Bernice.

I peer down at the picture again. Of course, Harry and I should've known better to think that we would be able to tell the difference between Madge and Lois in an old picture. When I had found Madge's body, I had thought it was Lois after all.

"Why did you cross out Lois's face then?" I bring Charlie's attention to the woman in the background who has been scribbled over.

"I didn't," Charlie says. "Someone else must've."

He steps away from the picture suddenly and rummages through the papers on his desk. In the flashlight gleam, dust particles swirl in the air like little mosquitos as Charlie flips papers over and lets some of them slowly float to the floor. He finally finds what he is looking for and reveals a scratched-up appointment book with a brown cork cover.

"I haven't told anyone this, but someone went through my appointment book. I know they did because I couldn't find it all last night or this morning before it conveniently reappeared on my desk sometime in the afternoon. At first, I couldn't figure out what they were looking for, but I've been thinking about it, and the only really important thing I have in here is an emergency list of medications and allergies for everyone who lives in the house. Lois gave it to me when I first moved in, in case anything happened. Maybe someone was hoping to poison Madge or give her a medicine that would poorly interact with something else she was taking."

"If they were trying to do that," says Harry, "why did they kill her with a knife?"

Charlie flips to the list he referenced and shows it to us. "Madge doesn't have any allergies, and she wasn't taking any known medicine at the time of her death."

"They wouldn't have been able to poison her like they had planned," I say.

"And whoever was looking through my appointment book must've crossed out Lois's face thinking it was Madge's," says Charlie.

"Wouldn't all of this information also point to Lois being innocent?" Charlie and Harry both turn their attention to me after I speak. "It wouldn't make sense for Lois to cross out her own face in a photo, and it also wouldn't make sense for her to need to look through the appoint book if she already had the emergency allergy and medications list."

"Or she would cross out her face because it makes her look innocent," says Charlie. "Also, for all we know, she could've lost her copy of the list and needed to use mine. Or maybe she was looking through my appointment book for something completely different."

Harry's eyebrows crinkle. "Why are you so quick to be suspicious of Lois?"

"Because Lois owed Madge a bunch of money, and Madge wanted her name on the deed of the house," I say, referencing both the information that I had found in the study and that Charlie had told me earlier. Two things that I hadn't bothered to share with Harry.

The whites around Charlie's black eyes grow. "Maybe she was looking for bank codes or something to try and get money."

"That's a strong possibility," says Harry. "An appointment book would be a good place to note such things."

Charlie places the appointment book back on his desk and glances down at a magazine that has fallen onto his desk chair. "The magazine I was looking for is right here!" he holds it up. The cover is dark blue and depicts a dinner table set with sparkling silverware and matching plates, not unlike the dinner table on the night Madge was murdered.

Chapter Seventeen

IN THE CELLAR

Back in the library, Charlie passes around the magazine so that everyone can take a glance at his friend's article. He does a good job of acting like nothing happened upstairs as he points to the colorful pictures of flamingos and filet mignon. Harry seems lost in thought though. His eyes keep darting over to me like he wants to talk to me in private. As the conversation comes to a lull, my eyes grow heavy and sting. I know I need to go to bed, but there's no way I'll be able to sleep in my room with the stench coming from the wardrobe.

Charlie lets out a theatrical yawn. "I think I need to retire for the night."

"Me too," says Bernice as she stands up from the heavily cushioned chair that she had been reclining in.

A loud slap of wind chooses that moment to crash into the side of the house, shaking it as if small tremors have been sent from the earth below. Rockey dives under the coffee table in the middle of the room while Rodeo lets out a long howl while rushing towards the French doors.

"I wonder if it would be safer for all of us to sleep in the library since it is on the lower floor," says Harry.

"I wouldn't be opposed to that idea," says Natalie. "This is one of the only rooms in the house that doesn't feel like a slab of ice." I catch a hint of sparkle in Natalie's blue eyes and can't help but feel like she's a little too excited about the idea of spending the night in the same room as Harry. I remind myself that as handsome as Harry is, I need to focus on solving Madge's murder and not dalliances with men.

"It's agreed then," says Bernice. "I can collect bedding, and we can all sleep down here. Maybe a couple of you could move the furniture around while I gather the linens?"

Harry, Charlie, and I rearrange the room to the best of our ability once Bernice leaves. Lois and Natalie also depart to go change into some more comfortable clothes to sleep in. In the end, we manage to create a space that should be large enough for five of us to sleep comfortably on the floor and one of us on the couch. Thankfully, the library floor is covered in a thick, antique rug that'll make sleeping without a bed a little more pleasant.

The fire is waning with only one small flame left. Charlie unties a few new logs and throws a large one into the fireplace. It lands in an awkward position and stifles the remaining flame. He bends down and rearranges the logs, but the fire has died down to embers. He then rummages around in his pockets.

"I can't find my lighter," he says. "I must've left it in the cellar when I went to get more wood."

"I can go and grab it," I say. I know Charlie has been doing well since his accident last night, but I don't think it's a great idea to have him overexert himself with so much running around.

"Is it that obvious that I have a migraine?" Charlies asks. "I feel bad having people doing things for me."

"I don't mind," I say. "I haven't seen the cellar anyway. It'll be a mini adventure."

"Because we all need a little more excitement today," Harry says before he cracks a smile.

The stairs to the cellar are down the hall and across from the study. Unlike the spiral staircase in the front hall with its exquisitely carved wood and craftmanship, the stairs leading down to the cellar resemble something similar to a child's attempt at home improvement. I take each step slow with one hand holding a flashlight and my other pressing against the crumbling wall so that I don't trip on my way down. The bottom of the cellar is unfinished. It's a hard concrete with little bumps and dips that have grown with time.

I point the flashlight around until I come to the triangular pile of wood across the room. There are a few abandoned spider webs at the edges of it, but right on top of the ligneous pyramid, there is a green lighter that Charlie must have left by accident. I slip it into my pant pocket when I hear voices talking above me.

"Where was the restaurant?" Harry's voice comes from the ceiling. It's slightly muffled but otherwise fully audible.

"It was just outside the city. Near the water," says Charlie, his voice also coming through fairly perceptible.

There's a quiet creak, and some of the dust from the ceiling unsettles around me as someone walks around the room above my head. I'm directly under the sitting area of the library. The insulation between the library and the cellar must be fairly poor.

"I think I've been to that one before," Harry replies. "It's a good date spot. I've taken quite a few girls there."

My cheeks flame in the dark. I'm really not in the mood to hear about all the women Harry's dated.

"It's also a good spot for dinner for one," Charlie says before laughing at his own joke.

I point my flashlight to the far corner of the room while mentally mapping the main floor in my head. If I'm standing below the library right now, that means the kitchen and dining room are to my right.

I get to the other side of the cellar and pause to listen. It doesn't seem like anyone is in the kitchen. There's another room in the cellar across from me with an open door. It would be below the dining room. No one should be in the dining room, but I guess it wouldn't hurt to check and make sure.

My flashlight spreads light around the cinder blocked room, and I see that this section of the cellar isn't empty like the main room. It's being used for storage. There are stacks of old boxes leaning against the walls with labels like *Christmas decorations* and *photo albums*. The boxes don't appear to have been touched in years based on the graying layer of dust that is starting to discolor the brown cardboard. In the far corner of the room, there's an old rocking chair with a moth-eaten throw tossed across it. I take a step closer and notice that unlike the boxes, the rocking chair doesn't have a thick layer of dust on it. Someone must have used it not too long ago. I pick the blanket up to fold it over the back of the chair when something tumbles from it.

A burgundy glove is on the floor. I pick it up, and it starts to drip water. Whoever wore this glove must've done so recently, otherwise it would be dry. I wring the glove out until it's only a little damp and put it in my pocket for safe keeping. I'm sure whoever dropped it wants it back, and I for certain want to find out who dropped it and what they were doing in the cellar.

One of the floorboards over my head creaks, and some dust settles down from the ceiling. Someone is in the dining room. I hold my breath, hoping they talk, even just to themselves, so that I can identify their voice, but it's silent. I wait a few extra minutes, but no more sounds come.

My flashlight flickers in the blackness. I can't keep waiting for whoever is in the dining room to speak or move again because my flashlight might die. It flickers again just as the thought passes through my head. Then, it goes out completely. I reach my hands out to one side and feel the dusty cardboard boxes. I can use them to help guide me to the exit of the storage room. Dust accumulates on my fingertips like some kind of crumbling icing as I move through the room. It takes a bit, but I finally find the hole in the wall that leads out to the main cellar. Unfortunately, it's just as dark as the little storage room. Because of the size of the main part of the cellar, it will be difficult to navigate my way to the stairs. I bang the end of the flashlight with the heel of my hand, thinking maybe that the batteries have only come loose, but the light remains dead.

If I walk straight, I could probably find the edge of the other wall and use that until I run into the woodpile, which I know is centered right across from the stairs. I step out into the darkness with my hands spread in front of me. If only I had counted the steps from the wall to the storage room in case something like this happened. I take another step, but the floor dips down, and I lose my balance and fall on my side while dropping the flashlight. My shoulder and arm cushion the fall as I hear the flashlight roll away until it hits something and stops. I've stumbled over the old concrete floor, and I have no idea what direction I now face.

CHAPTER EIGHTEEN

MADGE'S SECRET

There are a few loud creaks above me. If I call out, maybe the person will hear me like I can hear them. I open my mouth when a horrible thought strikes me. I have no idea who is above me. It could be Madge's murderer. The last thing I need to do is lure them into the cellar while I'm all alone in the dark down here. I'll have to come up with some other way to get out of here.

I shift how I'm sitting on the floor and feel something hard poke into my upper thigh. Charlie's lighter! I had forgotten it was the reason I came down here in the first place. I take it out and flick the little handheld device. A small flame jumps out from the top of it. While not as helpful as a flashlight, it still spreads a little bit of light through the room. I'm sitting only a foot away from the little storage room. There's a small curve in the floor in front of the door that must have been the source of my fall.

I get up off the floor and spot the firewood in the faint light. I head in its direction when a sound on the stairs catches my attention. Someone is padding down to the cellar. I close the top of the lighter in a flash and bend down near the wood pile.

"Emma, are you okay?" Harry's voice calls out.

I flick the lighter back on. Harry's standing at the foot of the stairs. He doesn't have a flashlight or candle with him, so he hasn't moved deeper into the room. There's a look of relief on his face.

"I didn't mean to startle you," he says. "You were gone for a bit, and I came down to see if you were alright. Where did your flashlight go?"

"It ran out of battery, and then, I tripped in the dark and had a hard time figuring where I was until I remembered I had Charlie's lighter in my pocket."

"For a moment I thought..." Harry trails off. "Never mind," he says.

"Thanks for coming and checking on me," I say.

"You must've taken a pretty good fall. It looks like the cut on your ear has opened back up."

Harry moves from his place at the end of the stairs until he's standing in front of me. He gently brushes my hair behind my ear. "You'll probably need to clean it up again."

I dab a finger to my ear, and it comes away with a drop of bright red blood. "I lost my footing when I was leaving the little storage room."

"Storage room?"

"It's off at the other end of the cellar. It's right below the dining room." I pause. "I actually thought I heard someone walking around above me when I was in there."

"Do you think they're still there?" Harry asks.

I shake my head no, but the movement causes my ear to throb. "No. I heard them leave. It was right after you and Charlie were talking about that restaurant by the water. The one that you like to take lots of girls to."

A streak of red stripes Harry's cheeks. "How did you know about that?"

"The ceiling isn't insulated properly. I could hear your conversation in the library."

Harry takes a moment to think. "We better be careful then when we're talking on the main floor. That means anyone down here could be eavesdropping like you were."

I cross my arms. "I wasn't eavesdropping on your conversation. You two were being so loud I happened to hear you through the ceiling."

A small smile appears on his face. "Whatever you want to call it is fine with me." He brushes my hair back once more. "We should probably clean up your ear. Let's get back upstairs."

In the kitchen, Harry finds the antiseptic and an old washcloth. He dabs my ear gently with the cloth until its clean. The alcohol still stings, but I try my best to pretend that it feels fine. I don't want Harry to think I can't handle a small scratch.

"It looks a lot better," he says while rinsing off the washcloth in the sink. "You're going to need to stop reopening the cut though if it's going to heal properly."

"Trust me, that's the first thing on my to-do list," I say. "Right after solving a murder."

"That's funny," Harry says. "That's at the top of my to-do list too."

I'm about to announce that I'm going to run up to my room and grab some clothing when a loud scream rings out into the night. Harry and I exchange looks.

"We better go upstairs!"

The two of us venture to the second floor where we find my bedroom door open and Bernice and Natalie hovering at the door's edges. Natalie's face has taken on a pallid color, and she covers her mouth with her gloved hand.

"What's going on?" Charlie asks. He's arrived just after us, presumably from the library.

I poke my head inside only to be greeted by the potent odor that has poisoned the air. Lois has opened the wardrobe and is staring at the stuffed vulture on the bottom of the shelf. Her large, green eyes water at the sight, and I'm unsure if she is about to cry or if the odor is just irritating. When I had originally decided not to share my knowledge about the toy vulture, it had been to avoid being associated with its discovery, but I hadn't thought about what would happen if someone else stumbled upon it.

"Who did this?" Lois says, her eyes scanning all of us hovered in the doorway. "Obviously, it's not a real vulture, but still, the message is rather disturbing!"

Lois picks up *The Vulture We Know* manuscript, being careful to avoid touching the dog toy. "Why would someone do this?"

The group of us by the door stay silent. Lois's green eyes study each of our shocked faces, but no one seems to give anything away.

"It's the curse," says Bernice. "I told you not to touch that manuscript."

Lois looks at Bernice. "It isn't the curse! I'm tired of the curse." Lois pauses for a moment before she goes on. "The curse isn't real, Bernice."

"Then how else do you explain everything that happens as soon as we start writing?"

Lois's cheeks turn red. "Madge."

"What?" Bernice says.

"She was behind everything. She was the curse." Lois's eyes are lit with a light so bright I can see the door to her mind opening to all of us in the room. "Why do you think I stayed with her all those years? There was something wrong with her. Ever since we were little girls, she had a fascination with the macabre. I tried to stamp it out of her, but it never worked. Whenever we picked up a writing project, I grew too consumed with the writing to keep a close eye on her, so she would get up to mischief."

Bernice's mouth hangs open before she speaks. "That doesn't make sense. Madge couldn't have caused an avalanche or a car to hit a post-man."

Lois bunches her hands into fists as she clings to the bulky fabric of her sweater. "She didn't cause those things. Those were just coincidences, but Madge caused the fires on set, the lost jewels when we filmed *The Day of the Green Leaf*, the small things. No one ever got hurt, so I never turned her in, but I kept my eye on her. There was no silly curse. It was just Madge."

"No one got hurt? What about that chandelier?" Bernice says. "A girl died!"

Lois shakes her head. "Madge had nothing to do with that. A few days before the chandelier arrived on set, I had caught her trying to steal a pair of shoes from the dressing room of the lead actress. I confronted her about it and saw her off on a flight home the next day."

"That doesn't mean she didn't get back on set," says Bernice.

"I had the same thought the day the chandelier fell, so I called our neighbors at the time to check on her, and they said she had been there and hadn't left since arriving home." Lois flexes her fingertips. "If I thought Madge had anything to do with that chandelier, I would've reported her. I tried my best to protect Madge, but even I have my limits."

Bernice silently stares at her friend of many years, taking in her bedraggled look. "I believe you, but that still doesn't explain the toy vulture in the wardrobe."

"Madge must've put it in here before she died," says Lois.

Bernice shakes her head. "That isn't possible. I checked the wardrobe for the manuscript shortly after Madge's death. I thought someone might've been after it. The vulture wasn't there that night. Emma and Harry were with me. They know it couldn't have been Madge."

"It's the truth. On the night Madge died, the vulture wasn't in my wardrobe," I say.

Lois sits down on my bed and squeezes her hands together. "Then who did this?"

"I think that's the question we've all been asking ourselves since Madge's death," I say.

CHAPTER NINETEEN

THE OTHER LANE

After Harry volunteers to dispose of the toy bird somewhere in the woods (the smell of the stuffed animal needs to be removed from the house—Charlie suggested that someone might have actually stored the toy among some dead fish), it doesn't take long to set the library up for our impromptu slumber party. Lois and Bernice have gathered enough linens and comforters from around the house to make a fluffy bed for each of us on the floor. I'm helping Bernice fold a comforter onto the floor when Harry comes up behind me and taps my shoulder.

"Can I have a word with you?"

Bernice eyes him warily and gives me a stern look before I follow him into the stacks.

His cheeks are striped red from the cold outside, and there's a small bit of stubble growing on his jaw from the late hour. He smells faintly of the woods and the cold winter air.

"When I went to bury the vulture, I found something. I think you should come see."

"How will we get away from the others?" I ask.

"I have an idea."

"Isn't the wind bad right now? Is it even safe?" I counter.

"There was a small break in the storm when I went out," he says. "It might last a bit longer if we hurry."

Out of the stacks in the main sitting area, Lois is fluffing a pillow on the couch, and Charlie is airing out some sheets that have been stored away for some time. Natalie and Bernice are shooing Rockey away from some of the bedding that has been thrown onto the ground while Rodeo watches near the fire, his tail happily wagging. Rockey seems to think that Bernice and Natalie are playing some kind of game, so he barks at them playfully. The two dogs must be excited to have so many people sleep in the library with them.

"Lois," Harry says. "Do you have a garden spade? I went to bury the vulture, but the ground is too hard to just use my hands. I think if we leave it uncovered, it might attract racoons because it smells so strongly of dead fish."

"We wouldn't want that," she says. "I don't know about a spade, but there should be a shovel out by the side of the house. We usually keep it there in the winter."

"Emma, come with me. If there's a bear or anything around, it's better to have two people," Harry gives me a wink when Lois looks away.

I nod my head in agreement, knowing full well that there aren't any bears outside, and grab my jacket off of the window seat before lacing up my boots. Outside, the wind has calmed, and there's only a breeze that lightly lifts up the small hairs that frame my forehead.

"We better make use of our time," says Harry. "Who knows when the wind will pick up again. The storm won't have blown through for a couple more hours if the radio is to be believed."

"Should we get the shovel?"

"No need," says Harry. "I found a deep tree well and put the toy vulture down there. I just needed everyone to think we had a reason for coming out here again without them knowing what we were doing."

Harry starts off in the directions of the woods, and I follow. Bernice's troubling eyes flash in my mind as I shadow each of Harry's steps. I've decided that I'm going to trust Harry, so I have to let the suspicions I have about him go. Harry and I reach the edge of the woods where's there's an opening between some fir trees.

"There's a dirt path just past here. Lois, Bernice, and Charlie might use it in the spring and summer, maybe even the fall. It's fairly well trodden."

Further into the forest, the plant litter below our feet thins, and a dirt trail comes into view. The woods are filled with noises of trees creaking in the breeze and unfamiliar rustles coming from just off the path.

"It's not far from here," Harry says.

The tree line thins, and the moon peeks out from behind the tilting branches. Harry stops in front of me when the path ends. A long, disused lane is in front of us. It has deep cracks and potholes, and in some places, there's more forest floor than pavement.

"Where does it go?" I ask.

"It connects to the main road and ends just a little bit up there." Harry points in the opposite direction of the road. "I think at one point someone thought about putting in a new driveway to *Nuthatch Nest* but changed their mind when they realized how much of a job it would be."

"I suppose I could ask Lois about it when we get back to the house. She won't wonder why I'm asking since I'm writing the article."

"Follow me," Harry grabs my hand and pulls me onto the lane.

We walk in the direction away from the road. Harry's hand is cold in mine, and his thumb taps against the joint of my own. He picks up his pace a bit. The drive is not sheltered like the woods, so wherever we're going, we need to be swift in case the weather turns again. Up ahead, there's a large shape sitting on the side of the road. It's cast in the shadows of the nearby trees, so I can't make out what it is just yet. Harry brings me closer, and then, it dawns on me.

"It's a car!" I run my hand along the trunk. "Whose though? Do you think Lois, Bernice, or Charlie would park their cars all the way out here?"

"There's an old carriage house up on the main road. I figure if any of them have cars, they probably park them in there. Not only that, but this road we're on right now is pretty washed out."

"If someone parks down here, it's because they don't want to be seen," I say.

"My thoughts are the same," says Harry.

"If my car is on the main lane, and yours and Natalie's are on the road, and Lois, Bernice, and Charlie, if they have cars, those are in the carriage house, then who owns this car?"

I peer through one of the car's windows and see that it's kept fairly neat. There's no telling trash or left behind sweatshirt that would indicate the owner is a man or woman. Other than something rectangular and flat with a metallic sheen lying on the backseat, the car is empty.

"It doesn't have any plates," says Harry.

I point to the backseat. "I think there's one in the back."

Harry stands next to me and peers inside the vehicle. He's close enough that I can feel the warmth of his body.

"The driver took it off because they didn't want people to see the plates. Why would someone do that?" Harry asks.

"Not only that, but who would do that?" I ask.

"There's only one person left who we haven't speculated about," Harry says.

"The dead man in my car?" I ask.

"Exactly."

"If he had his own car, why would he need to break into mine?" I trace my fingers over the hood of the car. This car is nicer than mine. It almost appears brand new.

"My guess is that your car was closer to the exit, and he was in a rush to get somewhere."

"Or leave somewhere," I say.

A great gust of wind pummels down the lane and pushes against my back. Harry stumbles a few inches forward and catches himself on the car.

"We better get going," Harry reaches for my hand and encloses mine in his own.

The tree limbs thrash in the air as Harry pulls me onto the path leading back to *Nuthatch Nest*. There's a large crack not far from the dirt path. Harry quickens his pace and tugs on my hand to keep up. Another squall bursts from above and shatters pine needles and tiny pinecones onto our heads. I run my freehand through my hair and try to pile the strands over my injured ear. I don't want anything hitting it for a third time and reopening the wound.

Up ahead, there's a small opening that marks the end of the path. With the help of another great gust of wind, Harry and I tumble out of the woods and into the open of Lois's backyard. Here, the wind is much worse. It tosses my hair left and right and batters at my head. I drop my hand from Harry's so that I can cradle my ear from the storm.

Lois's house is close. I can see the flickering light from the fireplace through the library windows. I focus on how the room will be warm enough to suck out the cold that's settled into my fingers.

Harry grabs my arm and roughly pulls me into his chest. There's a small rumble underfoot, and I see that a nearby tree limb has split from the trunk and landed right where I was standing.

"Thanks." I let out a breath.

"Falling limbs seem to be a theme around here. What is that, the third one that's fallen since you've been here?"

"It's the fourth if you count the twig," I say.

He smiles. "I think a twig would be categorized more as a digit than a limb." He grabs my hand. "Let's run for it."

We sprint across the lawn and manage to avoid another gusty punch by the time we get to the French doors of the library. Bernice is the first to greet us. She opens one of the doors widely for us and ushers us inside. She's wearing a blue robe and has piled her dark hair into a tall bun on her head. Rockey is at the door with her, his body wagging along with his tail in greeting to Harry and me.

"We were getting a bit nervous for a second," she says. "The two of you were gone longer than we thought."

"The wind had died down for a bit, so I guess we lost track of time," replies Harry. "We probably buried the toy bird a little farther away than necessary." He unzips his jacket.

I do the same. My fingers are warming with pins and needles shooting through them from the fireplace's heat. I gently pull the hair back from my ear and run a finger along the outer rim to make sure it's not bleeding. My finger comes away clean.

"We actually followed a path into the woods and found another road," I say as I pull my arms out of my coat. "Do you know what it's for?"

"Before I bought the house, the old owners wanted to build a guest house down that way, but I guess they changed their mind before construction started. The road was already put in, so they left it," says Lois. "No one uses it. When we first moved in, Madge would walk Rockey and Rodeo out that way," Lois's voice grows faint as one of her hands unconsciously strokes Rodeo on the forehead.

"It's in horrible shape too," says Charlie. "The last time I walked down there, the road was half washed away from some heavy rainstorms that we had in the spring."

"That's a far way to go just to bury a bird," says Bernice, her eyes locking on Harry's.

"I didn't want to attract animals up to the house, especially considering that there's a dead man in Emma's car," Harry replies.

A long silence follows Harry's remark.

"Thanks for taking care of the bird," says Charlie. "We'll have to air out Emma's room tomorrow once the storm ends. I can't imagine anyone wants the smell sticking around."

"I'm feeling pretty tired," says Natalie. She lets out a wide yawn.

"I do too," says Charlie. "I need to get some rest."

"I think it's time we all go to bed," says Bernice. "We've all had an exhausting day."

My own eyes are stinging with need for sleep, and my lids have grown heavy. A nice, long sleep sounds like the perfect thing right now. Both the couch and the comforter-made beds on the floor are tempting me to crash onto them. I glance up at Harry to see if he's sleepy too, but his eyes are staring at something out the window. His brows furrow together. He's so lost in thought that he doesn't even notice me watching him.

CHAPTER TWENTY

AN EARLY MORNING WALK

Once Harry and I have changed out of our outdoor clothes, we all draw cards, and it's determined that Lois will get to sleep on the couch. I'm assigned a spot along the wall with my feet resting up against one of the dog's beds. As I settle into my nest, my limbs feel like they are made of weighty stone. The soft sound of the fire eating at a fresh log and the heavy smokiness filling the air make it all the easier to close my eyes.

Before I drift off, my mind floats to Lois and Madge and the curse. For all those years, Lois refused to betray her sister to her best friend, even at the demise of her own career. I wonder if my own sisters, Kiera and Meg, would do the same for me. More curiously, how did Bernice factor into this equation? As much as she was protecting Madge, Lois was not only sacrificing her dreams to help her sister, but Bernice's too. Surely part of Bernice was writhing inside—incensed at Lois's choices and deception about the curse. Was it possible that Bernice knew about Madge before Lois's revelation? Had she patched the cloth together to form a tapestry that revealed Madge as the instigator of so many years of woe? Once she had figured it out, it would've been so simple for Bernice to attack Madge in the dining room.

The heaviness that lives in my bones lightens to foam, and I can feel my breath floating in my chest before my eyes delve into a darkness. I'm not sure how long I sleep for, but I know when I wake up it feels like cold fingers are pressing against my eyelids and the healing cut on my ear. I open my eyes and see my breath rise before me like steam. The library is freezing. The fire has burnt down to just the lightest orange embers winking in the dark. A cold breeze scatters my hair across my face and sends icy fingertips through my scalp and behind my ears. The French doors are wide open, and a full moon shines in through them, lighting the room in a cool blue hue. Why would the doors be open at this time of night?

I glance around me. The first thing I note is Lois sleeping gently on her side, her shoulders moving up and down with Rockey curled next to her. Right in front of the fire, Bernice lies on her stomach. Not too far away, Charlie is in the center of the room, spread eagle on his back with Rodeo spread out right over his head. The two makeshift beds of comforters and pillows closest to the door are empty. Natalie and Harry have slipped out into the night. Is it possible that what I sensed between them after their walk was a growing admiration, and the two have taken an opportunity to have some time to themselves? The thought makes me surprisingly jealous, so I remind myself that as attracted as I am to Harry, he's not my boyfriend, and I barely know him, so he and Natalie can do as they please. What if Harry and Natalie are up to more nefarious things though? I know I decided to trust Harry but disappearing in the middle of the night is a bit odd and a great way to lose someone's trust.

Navigating over the sleeping bodies is a bit of a game as I make my way towards the doors, but my gut is telling me the right thing to do is go outside and look for the two of them. I don't have my shoes with me, so the cold of the frozen ground seeps through my socks and kisses my feet when I step outside. Unlike the other night, no footprints can be found. A little bit off to the side of the door, a lone, burgundy glove is lying soiled on the ground. It matches the one I found in the cellar. I bend down and put it in my pocket before I head towards the path that leads to my parked car. The moon shines down on small limbs and the occasional roof shingle scattered on the ground from the windstorm that seems to be at an ebb. At the beginning of the path, the rusted gate has been torn from its hinges.

Before I can go any further though, I notice a figure standing at the end of the path. It's difficult to identify at first, but as my eyes continue to adjust, I make out Natalie's shape as she crouches behind several bushes.

"Natalie?" I whisper into the night.

Natalie startles and looks back at me. "Emma?"

"What are you doing out here?"

Natalie moves away from the bushes and joins me at the beginning of the path. "I woke up and saw Harry heading out here. I decided to follow him." She lets out a nervous laugh. "I know it's kind of stupid but curiosity got the best of me. I feel a bit embarrassed being caught playing detective."

"Were you watching Harry through the bushes?" I ask.

"Yes, he's been looking around your car with a flashlight. He's probably just playing detective himself," she motions for me to join her.

I peer between the mesh of needles and leaves and see Harry glancing into my car with a flashlight in hand. Harry moves towards the back of my car and pulls something out of his jacket that looks long and metallic, a crowbar? He approaches my trunk and uses the bar as a lever to pop it open. He steadies his flashlight and spends a few good seconds shining it into the trunk of my car before slamming it shut with a black gloved hand. He hides the crowbar back in his jacket before heading towards the path.

"What do you think he saw?" I ask Natalie.

Natalie doesn't answer. She pulls me aside into a crevice in the thick foliage, and we remain quiet as Harry walks past us. There's a great gust of wind, and I catch a whiff of Harry's woodsy scent as he moves by. He seems to be in a hurry to get back to the library. Once he's fairly far away, Natalie grabs my arm and pulls me back out of the shrubbery and motions for me to follow her back to the house. Out in the open of the backyard, the wind whips my healing ear, so I cover it with a hand. Natalie makes a swift retreat back, and I find it difficult to be quiet while I follow behind her. It's not until I'm standing on the threshold of the library that I realize my socks are clumped with natural debris. I don't have much time to dwell on it though because the commotion inside the library is enough of a distraction to forget about any mild physical discomfort.

Lois, Bernice, and Charlie (along with Rockey and Rodeo) have all woken up and appear disheveled in their sleepy states. Charlie has a patch of hair sticking up in an odd direction, and Lois has deep lines running across the left side of her face. Harry stands in the corner of the door, and his reentrance into the library hasn't gone unnoticed.

"What is going on?" Lois says, her hands clutching her arms in a self-hug to create some warmth.

"Why are the doors open and the three of you up?" Bernice adds.

Harry turns to look at us and realization registers across his face that he has been followed on his nighttime jaunt.

"Emma and I followed Harry. He was doing something with her car," Natalie says. There's a dark gleam in her eyes as she stares down Harry. She's pursed her pink lips together, and small lines have formed near them. Any perception of a crush that I perceived she might have had towards Harry is completely gone.

Harry is unusually quiet. He avoids our eyes and studies the floor.

"Do you have anything to say, Harry?" Bernice addresses him.

Harry is quiet a moment before he speaks. "Someone has disposed of Madge's body in the trunk of Emma's car."

"What?" Lois stands up off the couch before grabbing her head and sitting back down.

Bernice catches my eye before she speaks. "Why were you checking the trunk of Emma's car?"

"After we found the dead man in Emma's car, I thought that someone should take another look around for clues, so I went and checked."

"By yourself?" asks Bernice. "At who knows what time it is?"

"If you wanted to further look at the car, we all should've gone to-gether," says Charlie.

"He had a crowbar in his jacket too, like he had been waiting all day to just pop the trunk open," adds Natalie.

Bernice shakes her head. "I think it's time we all acknowledge that if Madge's body is in Emma's trunk, as Harry says, Harry would be the most likely person to have moved it out there."

"Me?" Harry takes a step backward.

"You are the fittest," says Charlie.

"Plus, you seemed to know exactly where to look for it," says Natalie.

"But why would someone move it?" asks Lois, still distraught over the displacement of her sister's remains.

Harry turns his eyes to me, pleading for me to do something, but there's nothing I can do. All the things that have been said about him are true. Out of everyone in the house, he would've had the easiest time moving the body, and it was odd that he would venture out in the middle of the night to break into my car. Something in my gut tells me to defend him though, or at least give him the opportunity to defend himself. He's been too good of an ally for me to jump ship. If he wanted to hurt one of us, he could have easily let the tree limb fall on me earlier or attacked me when we were alone in the cellar.

"Can you explain yourself?" I ask. "Natalie is telling the truth about us seeing you out there, so surely, you have a better explanation other than having trouble sleeping."

Harry runs a hand through his hair. "I had this strange idea that maybe that man we found in the car was the intruder that killed Madge. I thought that after killing Madge, maybe he had tried to get rid of her body by transporting it in the car, but before he could, he was killed by the tree falling on him. In order to know if my theory was right, I had to check to see if Madge's body was in the car, which, as we all know now, it is."

Bernice shifts under her blankets. "While that makes sense, it still doesn't explain your own behavior. You're running around here like you're a detective or something when we should all just be sitting tight, waiting for the power to come back, so we can call for help."

"Why would you be searching for her body anyway? Why would you think it had been moved from the dining room in the first place?" Charlie asks.

I avoid looking at Bernice before I speak. "Because the body was moved sometime last night or in the early morning. I caught Bernice coming out of the dining room yesterday morning, and she told me just as much."

"Is this true?" Lois looks at Bernice.

Bernice nods her head. "Yes. The whole thing had felt so surreal. I had spent that whole first night unable to sleep because I felt like I couldn't remember what Madge's face looked like. It was the most horrible thing—to forget the face of a lifelong friend. I thought maybe if I could just look upon her one more time it would settle my mind, but when I went to look, someone had cleaned the whole dining room." A lone tear escapes down Bernice's face. "Emma caught me as I was coming out, so I told her that the body was gone."

"Why didn't you tell us?" asks Lois.

"Because it was dangerous. Obviously, whoever moved it didn't want anyone to know, and I wasn't willing to risk my life or Emma's when a murderer was galivanting around the house!"

"This is quite a thing to not share with us," says Lois.

"You're one to talk about not sharing secrets," Bernice quips.

Lois quiets down as does the rest of the room. Rockey and Rodeo sniff at the cold air that's blowing in from the French doors that are still open. I go over to gently close them and double check that they're indeed locked. I don't think anyone wants any more surprise visitors tonight. Somewhere in the library, I can hear the sound of an old clock ticking away the seconds of silence.

Charlie is the first to speak. "While I'm not happy that Bernice and Emma kept this secret from us, we need to stay focused on what's happening around us and not let our emotions get in the way. Let's let Harry explain himself."

Harry takes a breath before continuing his story. "I knew about Madge's missing body too but not because I was sneaking around the library. I overheard Bernice's conversation with Emma about it."

"You were spying on us!" Bernice's eyebrows have pulled close together, and her eyes sharpen.

"I was on my way to my own room to change into a set of warm clothes when I heard you mention it to Emma on the stairs. What else was I supposed to do?"

"I suppose you heard the whole conversation then?" Bernice crosses her arms.

Harry's cheeks color red. "Yes, but I chose to try and pretend that I didn't hear the parts about how you thought I was the murderer and was seducing Emma for my own purposes. Those parts obviously weren't true."

"So, you learned that Madge's body was missing," says Charlie. "It makes sense that you would think it was in the trunk of the car. I think we've all seen enough movies to know that seems to be a popular place to put bodies, but it doesn't explain why you went to go look around the car in the middle of the night."

"It also doesn't explain the crowbar," says Bernice.

"I decided to investigate by myself because I didn't want to create a commotion over nothing. I realize now it wasn't the smartest thing. As for the crowbar, it was leaning against the house when I went out the French doors. I picked it up on my way to the car, thinking that it might be a handy way to open the trunk. I don't just carry crowbars around with me."

"I think we should all go look in the dining room," Charlie says. "I want to see for myself if Madge's body is gone. All these stories rely on he-said-she-said. I think we all ought to take a look for ourselves."

Bernice and Natalie agree quickly to this sentiment. Lois is slower to take up on it, not wanting to see the scene of her sister's departure. Harry and I follow the rest of the group out of the library to the dining room. As we walk down the corridor, Harry grabs my hand and gives it a squeeze before looking into my eyes. He looks exhausted with darkness framing his features, and his cheeks hollowing out the rest of his face.

"I need to talk to you in private sometime soon, not now though," he whispers just loudly enough for me to hear him. His breath leaves goosebumps up the backs of my arms.

CHAPTER TWENTY-ONE

WHEN THE LIGHTS TURN ON

We get to the dining room, and Charlie is the one to open the door as he holds the flashlight. The rest of us come in after him to view the scene. The dining room table is oddly set for a dinner party of five with full sets of sparkling silverware that create a nice contrast with the dark wood of the table, the true centerpiece of the room. The room is empty of the murder scene with the exception of a dark burgundy spot married to the carpet. Someone has definitely cleaned up and moved Madge's body.

Harry hovers near the table and takes a special interest in the utensils and table settings while Lois stirs uncomfortably near the doorway. I let my own eyes rest on the sideboard covered with the expired candles from the previous evening. Bernice sidles up next to me, and the smell of her flowery perfume tickles my nose so that it feels like I need to sneeze.

"Well, Harry, it looks like your story checks out," says Charlie. "I guess the mystery is solved then. It was an outside intruder the whole time, and justice worked its way into the world when that tree fell on him while he was trying to flee in Emma's car."

"Oh, Madge," Lois says. "I can't imagine what anyone would want with her."

"She probably just surprised him when he made his way into the house," says Charlie.

"Should we poke around the car to see if he took anything? Just to confirm the theory?" asks Natalie.

"It's best not to since the police will probably do that when they get here," says Harry. "I'm sure we'll all learn more about the man in the car once they identify him. He was probably just some common thief."

As if Harry's revelation hadn't already shed enough light onto the mystery, in that moment, the lights of the chandelier hanging in the dining room flicker and bask the room in an artificial light not seen since before the windstorm.

"The power!" Bernice clasps her hands together. "I'll go check the phone right now. Maybe we can finally call the police."

"I'm going to go check the thermostat to see the heat settings. This old house could use some warmth," Charlie says.

The dining room is even more beautiful now that I can see it in its full grandeur. The walls are covered in dark purple wallpaper with perfectly spaced sketches of roses. The purple of the walls helps to bring out the different hues found in the uncovered floorboards and other wooden furniture in the room, and the thick rug underneath the table has an intricate flower pattern sewn into it that ties the whole room together. It's hard to believe that such a horrid crime took place here just the other day.

"We better leave this room. Even though Madge's body has been moved, it's still a crime scene, and we don't want to accidently tamper with the evidence," says Harry.

In the kitchen, Bernice is just hanging up the phone as we enter. She drums her fingers against the nearby counter while she rubs her forehead.

"The phone line is still out. You would think that it would be fixed before the power," she says.

"We can still charge our cell phones though. I know service is spotty out here at best, but now that the weather is better, we could always give it a try," Charlie says.

Bernice lets out a huff of air and puts her hands on her hips. "Lois and I have always been very anti-cellphone, but after this debacle, I think we'll probably end up coming around to the technology revolution."

Charlie gives her a reassuring smile before disappearing out of the room. Shortly after, I make my way up to the second floor with Harry by my side. His fleece still smells a bit woodsy from the time he spent outside before the interrogation in the library.

"My phone broke yesterday morning when I was on my walk with Natalie, so do you mind if I help you find your charger?" he asks.

I nod in agreement even though I know he is just using an excuse to get a word in with me alone. I'm a little nervous about talking to him in private after watching him break open my trunk in the dark not too long ago, but I also feel confident that the six of us have managed to fit the pieces together about Madge's death.

In my room, it doesn't take long to find the phone charger and plug it into the wall along with my phone. My phone is completely dead, so it'll be a bit before it's up and running. Harry takes a seat on my bed and smooths over the few wrinkles that are appearing in his fleece. I take a seat next to him and try not to think about the state of my own wrinkled clothes.

"There were five steak knives on the table setting when we were in the dining room," he looks up at me, his brown eyes peering into mine with concern.

"But Madge was killed by one of the steak knives. Wouldn't the murderer have taken the murder weapon with him?"

Harry nods. "My thoughts exactly."

"So, you don't think that man in the car killed Madge?" I can feel my chest deflate. I thought that we had finally been able to wipe our hands of this mess.

"No, I think there's still a strong possibility that he did kill Madge, but I don't think he did it with a steak knife. I think Madge might've been trying to defend herself with the steak knife when he killed her with his own knife, something sharper, like a new or well-maintained pocket knife that he could've easily concealed on his body. Lois's steak knives are pretty blunt. I don't know how well they would've worked for a quick murder."

I shudder at his words. Like Lois's knives, they're a little too blunt for my liking. "Even if that's true, the mystery is still solved. That man killed her when she caught him intruding."

"We still haven't solved who killed him though."

"The tree killed him," I say.

Harry shakes his head. "Before you and Natalie caught me popping open the trunk, I managed to take a better look at him, and he had some wounds on him that didn't look consistent with a tree falling on him. If I were to guess, I would say he might've been strangled."

"Strangled!"

Harry makes a motion with his hand for me to quiet down before grabbing my hand. The heat from his palm sears my own, and I wonder if I would feel the same warmth if he were to trace the length of my fingers with his own.

"Listen, I think I have a full theory, but you can't tell anyone else," he says. "I think the man in the car killed Madge, and he was killed trying to get away with her body, but I don't think he was a thief who panicked when Madge caught him. I think someone hired him to get rid of Madge, and then, whoever hired him, decided to get rid of him too."

I bite my bottom lip. "Who would do that though?"

"Think about. Who do you think has the best motivation to do something like that?"

I think back to all the different clues that Harry and I have come across thus far. The clues all leading to Charlie didn't add up once we confronted him about the burned journal and peculiar photograph. And, while Bernice has a strong motive in terms of her dislike for Madge, she herself has appeared rather determined to solve the murder, and her reaction to Lois's revelation that Madge had been the perpetrator of the curse seemed genuine, which would make it unlikely for her to have killed Madge for that reason. Natalie is the person that I know the least about, but from everything that has come out in the past few days, she genuinely appears to be a person who has just been caught at the wrong place at the wrong time. To support that theory, she more than willingly shared her suspicions about Harry when she caught him fiddling with my car and didn't appear to have anything to hide.

That only left two people: Harry and Lois. I look into Harry's eyes and can't help but feel that despite the various suspicions I have against him, something in my gut keeps telling me to trust him. If I eliminate Harry, that would leave Lois as my only suspect. And, unfortunately, Lois is a good suspect. Not only has she spent her life trying to clean up after her sister's messy acts, she's also been entangled in financial mayhem at her sister's doing. Out of everyone in the house, she benefits the most from her sister's death.

"Lois has the best motivation," I say.

"I thought the same."

"What should we do?"

"I think we'll have to sit tight and keep our eyes on her until help arrives. If she's the culprit, she's had opportunities to hurt the rest of us within the past few days and hasn't taken them up, which makes me think as long as she thinks no one is on to her, she won't try anything."

"You're weirdly good at this detective thing," I say.

Harry smiles at me. "I read a lot of mysteries," he winks.

I smile back, and a small laugh escape my lips. I can't help but hope that after this whole thing is over, Harry and I will still stay in touch. It's not very often that a man catches my eye, especially while I'm trying to solve a murder, not that I solve murders often, or ever have before.

My phone lights up and awakens from its chargeless-slumber. I type in my password and check for reception bars on my home screen, but before I can, it goes black again, and the charging sign reappears. It looks like it still needs more juice.

"Weren't you and Natalie able to use your phones the night that you bumped into each other on the road?" I ask.

"No, remember we came down to the house to use the landline? The weather probably knocked out some of the cell towers like it did the ground lines. Once your phone has more charge, we could probably go to your car and see if we can find the spot where you last had reception."

"Sounds like a plan," I say. "Except for the fact that the last time I had reception, I was sitting where a dead man's body now rests."

Harry makes a face that lets me know he's not excited about the idea of shifting the body around, but he'll do what we have to in order to get out of this mess.

"There's another thing I need to tell you," Harry says. "Last night before I went to check on your car, I took some time to explore the other rooms in the house. I found myself in the study and found an interesting document."

"Did you find the receipt that stated Madge loaned Lois thousands of dollars?"

Harry shakes his head. "I found the deed to the house, and it didn't just have Lois's name on it."

"Madge's too?"

Harry nods his head. "Between what we know about Madge's mischief making and her demanding to be on the deed, it's tough not to point a finger at Lois."

"The one thing that still gets me is Lois's personality. She seems so warmhearted. She was more than happy to let me write an article about her house and offered rooms to you and Natalie without blinking an eye. I wouldn't expect a murderer to be so hospitable."

"Maybe that's why she did it though," says Harry. "Maybe she thought murdering Madge when the house was full of strangers would be the best way to cast doubt on herself."

"If that's true, then that night would've been the perfect opportunity for her to finally eliminate her sister."

I place my hands on my hips and feel a bulge coming from my one pocket. I put my hand inside and pull out the pair of burgundy gloves that I found near the library doors and the cellar.

"What are those?" asks Harry.

"Last night when I followed you and Natalie, I found one by the library door. It was near where we had found the footprints on the first night. The other one I found in the cellar."

Harry takes the gloves from my hand and studies them. "These match the scarf of the man who was in your car. It's the same material and burgundy color."

"He must've lost it when he was breaking into the house that night!"

"It would appear so," says Harry. "It's just more evidence that helps our theory that Lois hired him to kill Madge. If what we think is true, undoubtably Lois would've told him that she didn't keep the library doors locked, so he could make a fast entry and exit." He pauses. "I wonder why he was in the cellar though."

The answer comes to me quick. "When I was in the cellar, I could hear you and Charlie talking about a restaurant, remember? I could hear everything going on above me."

A stripe of red appears on Harry's cheeks.

"I bet the intruder got into the house through the library and hid in the cellar until he was ready to attack," I continue. "He would've known we were all in the dining room and kitchen area because he would've heard us from down below."

"Lois could've told him that the cellar was the perfect place to hide," says Harry, his face back to its normal coloring.

As helpful as this one-on-one conversation with Harry has been, I know it's best for us to get back to everyone else before they grow suspicious. The two of us make our way downstairs to the kitchen where Charlie struggles to reset a microwave clock based on the time on his wristwatch.

"It's only six in the morning," he tells us while pressing on various buttons. "Bernice and Natalie went up to their own beds now that the heat has been turned on. I'm not sure where Lois went. I'm a bit of an insomniac, so I probably won't be getting to sleep for a while. You two are welcome to stay up and keep me company." He finally presses the right buttons so that the microwave reflects the proper time. "Are either of you hungry?"

"I wouldn't mind something," says Harry.

Charlie pulls out several English muffins and expertly slices them in half before placing the halves in the toaster oven. He then proceeds to find a variety of jam and jellies in the side of the refrigerator door. They have exciting names on their jars like *Orangey Orange Jelly* and *Roasted Raspberry Jam*. I decide that I'll probably try the *Fruitious Fig Spread* first. It doesn't take the English muffins long to turn a nice golden color. Charlie sets them on the table and joins us in eating our morning snack. As predicted, the fig flavored spread is exactly what my taste buds need after so much excitement in the night. My body seems to melt into the flavor, finally letting go of some of the stress that I have been harboring these past couple days.

Charlie takes a large bite of one of his English muffin halves that has a yellow-colored spread sinking into the bread bubbles. "Before I reset the microwave clock, I checked the phone, and it was still dead. Once we're done eating, I'm going to check again."

Harry nods his head as he takes a bite of his own breakfast. He's chosen the orange flavored jelly. "Emma and I plan to look for reception outside once her phone has enough charge," he says. "It's still pretty windy, but it looks like it has settled down a bit, so we should be safe enough."

"Good morning," Lois greets us gloomily as she sways into the kitchen.

She's dressed in a pretty blue sweater with a matching knit scarf. She grabs an English muffin off the plate, and I take notice of her lithe fingers as they clasp the bread bun. Her joints have a swollen look about them that often accompanies hands that have worked hard in their younger years. I can't help but thinking that those very hands might've been used to snap the life out of someone just a few hours ago. She greets me with a warm smile that makes my insides cool.

CHAPTER TWENTY-TWO

A NOVEL START

Harry and I make our way up to my room to retrieve my phone after eating breakfast. The house is surprising quiet now that the wind isn't rumbling as much outside. We reach my room without running into anyone in the hallway, and the first thing I notice is that my phone is no longer sitting on the nightstand plugged into the charger. Harry looks as surprised as I am and checks on the floor beneath the bed but finds nothing.

"How long do you think we were downstairs?" Harry asks.

"Maybe twenty minutes? It couldn't have been too long because we were just buying time until the phone charged."

"Charlie was down there with us the whole time, and he was in the kitchen before we came back up here," says Harry, "so it couldn't have been him."

"It could've been Lois. Charlie said he didn't know where she had gone when we first got to the kitchen. She easily could've slipped into my room and taken my phone, especially if she overheard our conversation about her."

Harry pauses to think, staring at a corner in my room as thoughts weave through his mind. He runs a few fingers through his chestnut locks that appear a shade darker than they had the night we first met, most likely because neither of us has had access to a shower since then. I find myself wondering about my own appearance, aware that my dirty blonde hair probably looks a little more disheveled than I would prefer. As he thinks, I study his eyes and the intricate colors that build into the brown I've grown accustomed to these past few days. He has an occasional gold speckle hidden behind the dark hue. His eyes flick to mine as if he has an idea.

"We could go to Lois's room? That would probably be the most likely place for her to hide something she'd stolen."

I nod my head. "I'm not sure which room is hers though. I've been to Bernice and Charlie's rooms but no one else's room. Do you think there could be some way for us to ask for access to her room? Or get her to take us into it? That way there's no risk of her catching us snooping."

"That's a good idea, especially considering that we don't want to cast suspicion on ourselves."

I think of all the different reasons I could ask Lois to see her room. It can't be as obvious as my phone had been stolen, and I suspect she's taken it. The worn wardrobe comes into my vision, and I know I have the answer.

"We could ask her about *The Vulture We Know*. She must be working on the manuscript in her room since that's the only place in the house she would have complete privacy from Bernice and the others. We could ask her if we could read some of it!"

"Do you think she would let us?" asks Harry. "A lot of writers are protective over their work and don't like to show it off until they're ready. Plus, with Madge's death and all, I imagine she's probably not up to working on a new novel."

"Sometimes grief makes people look for distraction. It wouldn't hurt us to try."

"Maybe we could get Bernice to help us. I bet if we encouraged Bernice to get back into the project, Lois would be more than happy to share what she's written as long as her old writing partner is in the room. Now that Bernice knows the curse was just Madge's shenanigans, she has no reason to avoid helping Lois with *The Vulture We Know*." Harry cracks a smile. "I think that just might work. It's also not misleading as I would actually love to read *The Vulture We Know*."

"I thought your grandmother was the ultimate fan of B. Bookerton and L. Wrighter, not you." I give him a friendly smile back.

Harry shrugs his shoulders and lets out a little laugh. "I might be a fan myself, having read all their books."

I give his arm a light pat. "Let's go find Bernice and get this plan in motion."

Once we reach Bernice's door, Harry and I knock on it with a couple light taps. It doesn't take long for her to answer. She's wearing a gauzy white robe and has her hair artfully piled on the top of her head. She invites us inside to the sitting area of the room. Harry and I sit down on the dark gray love seat that has a yellow knit blanket thrown over its back. Bernice's room is surprisingly warm considering how long the power was off. She turns on a green tiffany lamp decorated in daisies and butterflies before taking a seat across from us in a gray reading chair.

"What a pleasure to see the two of you so bright and early." She takes a sip of coffee from a chipped cup steaming in her hands. "I should apologize to you, Harry. After reflecting a bit, I realize that I pegged you as suspicious a tad too fast. To think this whole time the six of us have been running around pointing fingers at each other when it was some random man is a bit embarrassing. It's such a relief now that the mystery has been solved."

Harry makes a dismissive gesture with his hand. "I can't blame you. I had my own suspicions these past few days."

"So, what brings the two of you by?"

"This might sound a bit crazy," I begin, "but we were thinking about your writing with Lois."

Bernice takes another sip of coffee before knitting her brows together. "What about it?"

"Well, after Lois admitted that Madge was behind the curse the whole time, it just doesn't make sense anymore for you and Lois not to be writing again."

Bernice sets her coffee cup on a coaster nearby and sighs. "I've had the same thought. I've just had mixed feelings about it. On the one hand, an excitement fills me to write again, but on the other hand, Lois did betray me to protect Madge."

"You and Lois have been friends for so long though, surely the good times must outweigh the bad?" I say.

"I suppose I could at least see what she's added to *The Vulture We Know* manuscript these past few days. Back when we were working on it together, it had been my favorite story so far." Bernice's eyes cloud over wistfully. "Lois will probably feel up to it too. She always took to writing when things in her life were getting difficult, and losing Madge is one of the most difficult things that's ever happened to her."

Bernice guides us to a door on the second floor and knocks gently. The inside of Lois's room is like nothing I've ever seen before. The walls are painted a soft yellow with silver crown molding. Lois's decorative choices are full of bright colors. Her comforter is fuchsia and complimented with large orange and yellow pillows that sit atop her bed. Her room is set up the same way as Bernice's, except instead of the gray furniture that Bernice is so fond of, Lois has selected a smorgasbord of eclectic findings that range from a purple and white polka-dotted couch to a thread-bare arm chair with bits of scaly-looking fabric.

Lois is sitting at a faded green desk situated next to her bed. She's bent over several pieces of paper and scratching at them with a pen. When she hears us enter the room, she looks away from her work, somewhat startled.

"Hello," she says welcoming us to her room. "I wasn't expecting anyone to stop by. Did we finally get the telephone line working?"

"Not yet," says Harry.

I study Lois's face to see if there's a hint of relief that the phone still isn't working, but it doesn't betray anything.

"This is just awful. I do hope the issue gets resolved soon," she slings a wrap over her shoulders. "If only I had a cellphone, then I would try to make the call myself."

"Are you working on *The Vulture We Know*?" Bernice asks.

Lois lowers her eyes to the floor. "I am. I know we fought about it, and you don't agree with me working on it, but I really think that it's time to pick the pen up again." Lois takes a deep breath. "I'm also sure that you would understand that I am in need of a bit of a distraction right now."

"I think it's time we start working on it again as well," says Bernice.

Lois raises her eyes in surprise. "You do?"

Bernice nods. "Yes. Like you said, the curse was never real. It was just Madge. There's no reason for us to avoid writing any longer."

"Yes, Madge..." Lois's voice trails off. She recollects herself along with some of the papers on her desk. "Let me show you what I have so far."

Bernice joins her at the desk, and to my surprise, Harry follows in her wake. I guess he wasn't joking about being a big fan of their work. I'm left alone near the doorway to glance in the corners and peruse the room with my eyes for signs of my phone. There is a dark rectangle shape resting on a side table by the polka-dot couch that catches my eye. I inch towards it only to realize that it's a jewelry case and not my phone. The shine of the black case in contrast to the dusty table top makes me pause. The jewelry case must have been recently used.

Over by Lois's desk, Lois explains something she has done to the syntax of her work while Bernice and Harry listen vividly. I snatch the case and lift the lid. Inside, one sapphire earring with a silver backing is set against the faux velvet of the case. Breath catches in my throat, and I close the top of the jewelry case quietly. Why would Lois have Madge's earring in her room—the same earring that matched the one I had found in my own room the night Madge died?

Lois could've easily snuck into my room when Harry and I were downstairs and ransacked the wardrobe, looking for *The Vulture We Know* manuscript, and then, she could've snuck back into her own room before Bernice got there. Why would she ransack her own wardrobe looking for a copy of a manuscript that she already had though? There must've been something else in the wardrobe that she wanted. She must've been in a hurry too, which means that whatever it was that she wanted from the wardrobe, it was something that she didn't want others to find.

I glance up just in time to see Lois, Harry, and Bernice retreating from the desk and heading towards the door. I join them easily as they continue their discussion.

"Your new ideas are just marvelous," says Bernice. "I'm going to head to the kitchen to grab some more coffee and a bit to eat. Lois, I think we should go together and spend some time brainstorming. I haven't felt this way in years."

Bernice links her arm into Lois's, and the two make their way down the stairs, their shadowy forms retreating from Harry and I in the hallway. Once they're officially out of sight, I let Harry know that I didn't find my phone, but I did find the mate to the earring I found in my room.

"What do we do now? Without a phone on hand to contact the authorities, I don't think confronting Lois is the right move. She could be more dangerous than she appears," I say.

Harry turns to me with an intense stare that wraps his face in urgency. "We need to go to the library," he says.

CHAPTER TWENTY-THREE

THE BUTLER'S PANTRY

Rockey and Rodeo are sprawled on the couch when Harry and I get to the library. Rockey in particular seems to be having quite the dream as his paws twitch and snout wiggles. The most surprising sight though is that someone has put the library back to the way it was before our untimed sleepover last night. The stiff looking twin chairs, with their backs to the window seat, are facing the coffee table, and the old armchair is in its corner by the fire.

Harry must have the same thought. "Natalie and Charlie must've put everything back."

"Why did we need to come to the library?" I ask.

Harry glances over at me with an odd look in his eyes. "I need to go through Lois and Bernice's books. When Lois was showing *The Vulture We Know* to me and Bernice, I had this weird idea." He ruffles his hair, something I notice he does when he's a bit nervous. "They've written a lot of books, so I was thinking you might be able to help me."

"Sure, but you'll have to tell me what I'm looking for."

"To start with, we need to collect their books and put them in order of publication date. Right now, the books are shelved together, but their organized alphabetically."

Harry leads me to a bookshelf with a section filled with jeweled colored spines. They all bear the words *B. Bookerton* and *L. Wrighter* in metallic script. I glance over the array of novels that looks like it goes on and on. I really hope whatever idea Harry has doesn't lead to a dead end.

"Harry, there are a lot of books here. It'll take us a bit to flip to every publisher's page and find the publication date."

"I guess we better get started then," he hands me the first book on the top shelf titled *Abridgement of Ruby Flowers.*

The two of us get to work, settling on a system in which we organize books into decades before finally placing them into numerical order once we think we've gathered all the books that belong to a specific era. At first, it's fun to read the titles like *Rain Drops on the Orange Chrysanthemums* and *A Snow-Covered Street in Twilight Moons*, but after a while, the titles all blur together into nonsense words and phrases.

Around the time that the edges of my thumbs go numb from excessive page flipping, Harry and I hear the faint sound of one of the library doors opening. I carefully set down the book I've been looking at, *Storms and Rivers in the Western Fields*, and pop my head out from between the bookshelves to see who has come into the room. Charlie is standing near the doorway holding a tray of what smells like freshly made food. He smiles at me as the spices dance under my nose, and my brain conjures up images of Mediterranean salads and Italian breads.

"I thought you might want something to eat since it's almost lunch, but I couldn't find you," he walks towards me with his tray, but I scamper out of the shelving area and meet him closer to the door.

"I actually wanted to talk to you about something in the kitchen," I say, guiding him back out into the hallway. I'm still not exactly sure why Harry wants to sort all of Bernice and Lois's books, but I have a feeling that he doesn't want the whole household to know what he's up to.

"What about?" he asks.

I dig my eyes into the wallpaper decorating the hallway as if it somehow holds the answers to all my questions.

"I wanted to talk about the phone," I say quickly.

"The landline is still out," he says. "I know you and Harry were planning to go and find cell reception somewhere outside, but since I didn't hear anything from either of you, I just figured it hadn't worked."

The two of us arrive in the kitchen, and Charlie places his silver tray on the kitchen table. Someone has put a blue picnic cloth over it along with a stack of cream-colored plates. My stomach gives off a light growl as I study the freshly sliced tomatoes and mozzarella cheese that has olive oil drizzled over them.

"We actually didn't get the chance," I glance away from the food. "It turns out I completely misplaced my phone."

Charlie's lips pull down, and a small dimple appears in his chin. He grabs my arm and pulls me closer to him. "Mine is gone too. Someone took it from my room."

My eyes widen. "You mean someone stole yours too?"

He nods at me. "Obviously, someone doesn't want us calling for outside help. The reason I haven't strayed too far from the kitchen is because I don't want anyone trying to do something with the landline."

"I can't believe this."

"Me too," Charlie grabs one of the nearby tea towels and bunches it in his hand. "I thought we had solved this whole thing when Harry figured out the man in your car must've killed Madge."

I nod complacently. I haven't forgotten that the suspicions Harry and I share about Lois are only between the two of us. As far as Charlie and the rest of the house's residents are concerned, the mystery has been put to rest once and for all.

"How's your head been since the night you fell?" I feel bad not having asked about it sooner.

Charlie looks as relieved as I am with the subject change. "I think I'm all better. It's the weirdest thing though. I keep thinking that I'm starting to remember something important. It's like having a word on the tip of your tongue, and then suddenly, poof, the memory just disappears."

"Is it anything in particular that you think might be coming back?" I ask.

"That's the thing," Charlie shifts uncomfortably. "I keep seeing Madge leave the room."

"What do you mean?"

"It's like a flashbulb moment. I see her head just bobbing past the opening of the kitchen into the hall as if she's headed towards the dining room, and then, it goes black."

"If Madge was walking away from you when everything went dark, wouldn't that suggest that someone could've struck you while you were watching her?"

Charlie takes a pause before continuing, "What if someone hit me, but they were going for Madge and missed somehow?"

Charlie points to a door that blends in with the rest of the kitchen. "The pantry is large enough for someone to hide in. It's possible that

they spotted Madge through a crack in the door, and then, they retreat-
ed back inside to get ready to pounce, but when they jumped out, they
ended up miscalculating the kitchen layout and hit me instead while
Madge was in the hall."

"Would they have hidden in the pantry after they hit you too?" I ask.

Charlie shrugs. "That I can't know seeing as I was knocked out."

"Have you checked the pantry for clues?"

"I have, but because it happened so many days ago, and people have
been in and out of the kitchen enough, any clues have probably been
disturbed."

Charlie's dark eyes, the color of moonless midnights, hover over the
pantry door lost in thought. Is it possible that Lois struck Charlie by
mistake, so she hid in her own pantry? I think back to that night, but
the whereabouts of everyone is a bit fuzzy. I know that I was alone in
the dining room when Madge yelled for help upon discovering Charlie,
so the locations of the rest of the guests is tough to calculate.

I leave Charlie in the kitchen after a quick bite and return back to the
library. Harry is gone, and the books have been shelved back into their
alphabetical order as if we had never disturbed them in the first place.
Harry must've finished his quest and found whatever information he
needed from the novels. I traipse into the main part of the library which
is equally empty. Rockey and Rodeo watch squirrels outside and paw
against the pane at a bird who is hopping too close for their liking. I give
the bird a better glance myself and discover that the two mutts have
in fact found the mysterious nuthatch. Its cream chest is puffed out in
contrast to its tiny black marked head that bobs along as it searches for
seeds on the ground. It must be hard being a bird in the winter while
having to rely on leftovers and scraps. It's not unlike trying to solve a
murder mystery with just a few random clues. Rockey lets out a loud

bark, and the nuthatch takes flight into a nearby tree before hopping away into thicker foliage. Rockey turns back to give me a disappointing look as if it's my fault the bird has disappeared.

"I'm just as bummed about the bird leaving as you are, buddy." I give him a tender pat on the head.

I shift on my feet and step on something small and round. I bend down to see what it is, and mistake it for Natalie's dark pearl earring before realizing it's only some left behind food crumb. Rockey manages to scarf it up before I can stop him. He toddles away to his bed while licking his lips.

I take a seat on the couch and stare at the emergency radio set up on the coffee table. I can't help but wonder if Lois has a television somewhere in her house. It would be nice to get a visual on how bad the wind has left the roads since we might have to take to them and hike to the nearest police station or public place with a working telephone now that the storm has been dying down for a few hours. I can't imagine us holding out here much longer after so many horrendous developments. Charlie is probably the best person to ask about the TV, and he's exactly where I left him at the kitchen table just moments ago. He's nursing a cup of what looks to be green tea, based on its color, and flipping through a food magazine. He's enchanted by a picture of banana foster when I take a seat across from him.

"I once visited a college town in the Appalachian Mountains, and the dining hall had the best banana foster. It was the oddest thing," he flips the page of the magazine where another picture of the fruity dessert appears. "I should've written an article about it. It's the trending dessert now."

"I don't think I've had it before," I say.

Charlie raises his eyebrows. "I'll have to make it for you sometime. It's delectable." He smooths his straight, dark hair on top of his head. "I take it you didn't come back into the kitchen to talk about desserts though?"

"Does Lois have a TV?" I ask. "I thought it might be helpful to watch the news and see what's going on out in the world. Of course, that's only if her cable is working. Things not working tends to be a theme around here lately."

Charlie flips another page in his magazine. This time it's a picture of banana foster sitting in a bowl with so much sauce it looks more like a banana soup than a dessert. Charlie makes a face and holds the picture up to me. "Innovation is wonderful, but don't fix something that's already perfect." He closes the magazine. "And to answer your question, I'm not aware of a television set. And if she does have one, she probably doesn't pay for cable, so the news probably isn't an option."

"I feel like we've come to a bit of a standstill," I say.

I study Charlie as he runs a finger across the glossy cover of the food magazine. Is it possible that Lois does have a TV, or internet, and Charlie is just buying time because he's somehow connected to the murder? Behind Charlie, the landline rests on the kitchen counter. It's made from a cantaloupe-colored plastic that ages it well. If I were to pick it up right now, would I be greeted by a friendly dial tone?

Charlie leans towards me conspiratorially and drops his voice. "I keep thinking about our conversation earlier, the one about the intruder possibly hiding in the pantry. I think I might've come up with a theory that explains a few things."

I sit up straighter in my seat. Charlie's theory could be an essential clue to solving what happened to Madge. He stands up and makes a gesture for me to follow him towards the pantry.

"At first, I thought I was going crazy, but then I remembered this one book of Lois and Bernice's called *Rain Drops on the Orange Chrysanthemums*. Have you read it?"

"No, but I recently became familiar with that title," I say a bit ironically, thinking back to stacking books with Harry in the library just moments ago.

"Well, that book is all about secret passages. I thought to myself, *Nuthatch Nest* is pretty old, it's a historical site, maybe it has some old passageways that've been sealed up."

My eyebrows automatically rise at the idea of there being a secret passage in Lois's house. While I do admit that the house is old and probably has lots of secrets, the thought of one of those being a hidden passage is too much of a stretch for me.

Charlie blows his cheeks out and lets out a sigh of air. "I know the idea is one that only a lunatic could come up with, but I thought, what does it hurt if I give it a try? If I don't find a secret passage, I'll just never tell anyone that the thought traveled through my head." Charlie's eyes glance over at the pantry door. "Anyway, I'm telling you about the thought right now, so you can probably draw your own conclusions."

"You found a passage?"

Charlie opens the pantry door, and I follow him inside. While it is well stocked with canned food and other nonperishables, the pantry has the faint musty smell of abandonment. Charlie grabs at one of the pantry shelves and gives it a hefty pull. I jump back to avoid the ricochet of Charlie's elbow, but instead, the whole pantry wall gives way, and the scent of must completely envelops the air around us. I can't believe my eyes. There's a small hidden room just beyond the pantry. It's empty with the exception of a barren, built-in shelving unit for wine. Small nuthatches have been carved into the side of the shelving in a delicate hand.

"This must've been part of the original house. Someone has carved little nuthatches into the shelving," I say.

"They must've remodeled the kitchen at some point in time and decided to semi-seal up this room because it wasn't being used," replies Charlie.

"Did you figure out where it leads to?" I ask.

"It's a butler's pantry, so I figured it was to the dining room, and I was right."

He enters the small space and pushes firmly against the opposite wall until it swings open in a similar matter to the one in the pantry. Charlie and I are standing in the dining room, almost directly in front of the spot where Madge's body once rested. Behind us, I see that to get access to the butler's pantry from the dining room side, someone would need to know that an old bookcase would lead the way.

"Whoever built this thing wasn't thinking too much about the type of entrance this door would make. I imagine that if someone popped out of here, they would really give whoever was in the dining room quite the scare."

"The hidden butler's pantry also explains how the intruder was able to disappear so quickly after attacking Madge. He must've gone into the passage and waited until it was safe to move her body," Charlie says.

"So, we know how the intruder managed to flee the scene of the crime so quickly, but how did he move Madge's body in and out of the house without making any noise?"

"Maybe through the library? Last night when the three of you disappeared out the French doors, Lois, Bernice, and I didn't even wake from our sleep. Those French doors are well oiled, and those rugs are plenty thick. Plus, say if everyone was upstairs when the body was moved, we would be even less likely to hear anything.

"Hello?" a distant voice calls out from the other end of the pantry.

Charlie's eyes grow wide, and we swiftly head back through the butler's pantry. Charlie's shoe skids on some loose dirt as we hurry back into the kitchen pantry, so we end up making a bit more noise than intended. We make sure to close the door that leads to the butler's pantry fully so that it's disguised back into a plain shelving unit. The two of us exit to find Lois standing in the kitchen with a concerned look on her face.

"What were you two doing in there?"

"Trying to figure out what to make for dinner. I was convinced we had some canned salmon somewhere, but I couldn't find it. Emma volunteered to help me, but she couldn't find it either. I guess we won't be having salmon salad sandwiches." Charlie closes the pantry door behind him.

Lois seems to accept this explanation and busies herself over the stove by pouring a cup of hot water for some tea. I glance up at Charlie who swiftly raises his eyebrows at me before returning to the magazine he had been reading earlier. It appears that Charlie doesn't believe in Lois's full innocence despite Harry putting forth the intruder theory. Is it possible that he too made the same connections we did about her? And if so, what information does he have that Harry and I don't?

Chapter Twenty-Four

TWO SILVER NUTHATCHES

I reach the top of the landing on the second floor and let out a small huff. It's more work getting up and down the spiral staircase than it looks. I need to find Harry and tell him about the hidden butler's pantry that connects to the dining room. He'll have some ideas of how it could be connected to the murder. I am halfway down the hall when I remember that Harry told me his room was closest to the stairs. I knock on the door and wait for a response. There is none, so I knock once more. He might be ignoring the knock, thinking it's Lois or someone else he doesn't want to talk with. I turn the knob and enter the room.

Harry's room is a similar size to mine and fairly spartan. His bed is nestled against the far corner and messily made. He must only sleep on one side based on how smooth the one half of the bedding is compared to the other. Opposite of the door, there's an old window that's not closed all the way. It looks to be stuck based on the lopsided position of the pane. Harry's room must be much chillier than mine at night.

Unlike my room with its large wardrobe and small nightstand, Harry's room has a large set of drawers and a writing desk. There are papers scattered all over the desk in disarray. I take a step closer and peer at some of the writing. He's been keeping notes about the case. He has paragraphs under Lois's name of important things the two of us have found out about her. He's really taken to playing the detective. I pick up the page on Lois and flip it over. On the other side I see the names of the rest of us listed out. Under Charlie, he's listed the photograph he discovered and scratched through it. He probably did so after we asked Charlie about it. I skim down to my name to see what he's listed about me. There's only one line written under my name, and it's a question: *Why doesn't she know more about Lois, her Great Aunt?*

My cheeks heat. I'm happy I'm not a prime suspect on his list or, really, a suspect at all, but it is a bit embarrassing that he jotted down some notes about me. I put the paper back where I found it when my eye catches something else. A small pack of yellow disposable cameras are on the edge of the desk. One camera is missing as if Harry has taken it out to use. I haven't seen disposable cameras like this in ages. I don't even know where someone would purchase a pack of them or get the film developed anymore.

There's a heavy knock from Harry's door. I freeze. Who could that be? Surely, Harry wouldn't knock on his own door. I try to be as quiet as possible, but another knock follows. Slowly, the door handle turns clockwise. I leap across the room and grab it, holding the door shut and the knob still, praying that whoever is on the other side just thinks it's locked. The knob stops turning and pressure is let off of the door. The sound of footsteps retreats. My heart is beating so fast it might as well have jumped into my throat. I should leave Harry's room. There's not much else to look at, and I don't need people to start casting doubt on my own innocence.

I exit Harry's room and try to close the door quietly, but it ends up slamming, causing an echo through the hall. The window must have created some kind of vacuum and caused it to shut rapidly.

"Who's that?" Lois calls from the stairs.

My heart quickens. The last person who needs to see me sneaking around is Lois. I hear her steady steps creaking up the stairs towards the second floor. I move to open the door next to Harry's when I remember its Lois's bedroom. I scamper to the next closest door and throw myself inside the room as silently as possible.

"Is anyone here?" Lois asks from the hall. "Must be the wind making sounds again," she says to herself. I hear her enter Bernice's room.

I let out a steady breath. I need to be more careful. This is the second time I have almost been caught. Had Lois known what I was doing, things could've been bad. I realize I am standing in the room that Harry and I thought was empty on the first night. It has an odd odor in the air, similar to stale flowers. The only thing I can see in the room is the outline of what must be a thick set of curtains blocking out the afternoon sunlight. I move towards the curtains and edge them open. The view outside is of the walking path leading to the lane. This must've been the room that I saw someone peaking out of on the night I first arrived. With the curtains now open, I can see more of the area. It's a small room like mine and Harry's, but it has more furniture and appears lived in. The bed has a blue quilt neatly folded on its end, and next to the door, there's a table with a vase of roses under a light switch. I lightly smack my hand against my head. I had forgotten that the power had come back on. Instead of crossing the room, I could've just turned on the light.

On a chair by the bed, a small pile of clothes has been neatly stacked. Most of the clothing is a shade of blue. There is an azure dress stacked on top of some navy-blue trousers followed by a pair of dark blue socks. This must be Madge's room. Similar to the dining room, I imagine Madge's room will be of great interest to the authorities when they arrive, and the last thing I want is to go around and touch all her things. I go to close the curtains when something placed on the nightstand grabs my attention. There's a white envelope with my name scrawled across it: *Emma Finch*. I reach for the envelope and tuck it under my shirt. Normally, I would never take something from someone else's room, but considering that Madge's dead, and my name is written on the note, it's for the best.

Out in the hall, I hear a door open and footsteps. Lois must be back out there. I lean my head against the door and listen. It sounds like she's fiddling with some candles on the sideboard. I take the envelope out from under my shirt. It's unsealed, so it's easy to slip the letter out. I unfold it and frown. The letter is unfinished. All Madge has managed to write is a salutation and a couple sentences:

Dear Emma,

Lois recommended I write you a letter to welcome you to <u>Nuthatch Nest</u>. I was not on the best terms with your Uncle Albert, but I will try to put that aside for now for the sake of your article on this beautiful house. I suggest you take a great interest in the study. It is one of the rooms in the house closest to the original and filled with...

Filled with what? Clues to who murdered her? That wouldn't make sense. There's no way Madge knew that she was going to get murdered. There must be something of historical significance in the study.

I put the letter back in the envelope and place it back under my shirt. There's no point in leaving it in Madge's room. Outside, the hall has finally fallen quiet. I creep out of Madge's room and silently close the door by not letting go of the handle until its completely shut, remembering the loud bang Harry's door had made.

I need to make my way to the study. I know that Madge's letter can't be about her murder, but if there is something in the study with a great historical value, it could be an important clue that will help Harry and I fit everything together.

When I get to the kitchen on my way to the study, Charlie is hanging up the phone.

"Still nothing," he says. "Where were you?"

"Just upstairs," I say. "I'm going to go to the study. It was hot up there."

"Can you grab me something from in there?" he asks.

"Sure," I say.

"Last time I was in there, I left my reading glasses. I don't normally need them, but this one article I've been reading has some footnotes that I just can't make out. They're just a pair of black, rectangular frames."

"I'll bring them right back," I say.

"Thanks," says Charlie. He goes back to reading a culinary magazine that's spread out on the kitchen counter top. The article is about the different ways to incorporate gourds into various lasagnas.

I get to the study without running into anyone else on my way. I feel more comfortable in here knowing that it is not considered a private area like Harry and Madge's bedrooms. Now, what could Madge have wanted me to see in the study? I peer down at the coffee table book again, but that seems like too mundane a thing to point out to me. Plus, whatever I'm looking for must have been part of the original house, and I doubt the coffee book was published in the 1870s. There is something stuck in the tome though, causing it's cover to bulge out just a bit. I open the book to where the pages separate, and I find Charlie's reading glasses. He must've been flipping through the book when he left them here.

Before I close the book, I pause once again. The page Charlie has left his reading glasses on is about *Nuthatch Nest*, but it's a section I haven't read yet. It's titled: *Ralph Swanhild and Family Portraits*. On the page, there's a collection of three paintings. The first one must be Ralph himself. He has a long white beard and great, bushy eyebrows that sweep into his eyes. His face holds a bit of a sour expression. He isn't exactly what I was picturing in my head when I imagined a romantic widower building a mansion in honor of his beloved. The next painting is of a young woman with large green eyes and is captioned: *Hester Swanhild*. She's wearing a dark green dress that's fitted on the top, and in the background, a white-breasted nuthatch flies over her head. She must have asked the artist to include the detail of her favorite bird.

The last portrait on the page is of a wedding. A young bride, Hester, stands next to a Ralph Swanhild. Hester holds a small bouquet of white lilies in one hand while the other is clasped to her chest, holding something that I can't exactly make out. Ralph stands next to Hester, one hand set firmly on a cane, and the other placed on his chest, mirroring Hester's pose. His hand is holding something too. I move closer to the portrait, but I just can't figure out what either of the objects are in the painting. I need something that will let me study the portrait better.

Charlie's reading glasses rest to the side of the book. I have not used readers before, but I figure they must work somewhat similar to a magnifying glass. I slip on the glasses and take another gander at the portrait. Hester seems to be holding a tiny figurine of sorts, but I can't quite make out its shape. Ralph seems to be holding the same, but less of his hand is covering it. I stare at it for a minute when it hits me. The two are holding tiny, silver nuthatches. They must have been some sort of wedding gift.

I take Charlie's glasses off of my nose. Had Charlie been looking for the same thing as I had when he used his readers to study the page? Or had he simply been curious about the portraits. Besides that, something about the silver nuthatches is bothering me. They look rather familiar, but there's no way I would've seen them before.

I flip the page of the book and find that there's another bit about *Nuthatch Nest*. As if the book knew what I wanted to know, there's a whole section titled *Silver Nuthatches*. I scan the text until I find what I'm looking for.

On Ralph and Hester's wedding day, Ralph gifted Hester two solid silver nuthatches, one for each year that he'd known her. He would later go on to incorporate the silver nuthatches into *Nuthatch Nest*, including creating two replicas (not made of solid silver) to serve as door knockers. The whereabouts of the original silver nuthatches are unknown, but they are believed to still be part of the original house.

That's why the nuthatches had looked so familiar. They were identical to the house's door knockers. I wonder what happened to the originals though? Surely something made of solid silver that was incorporated into the house would be easy to spot?

I glance around the study. Maybe Madge thought I would enjoy seeing the silver nuthatches and learning about the love story behind them for my article? The little nuthatches could be incorporated somewhere in the study. After all, the letter did imply that the study hadn't been tampered with over the years. I run my hand over the antique globe between the two chairs. Where would Ralph put the nuthatches?

My thoughts wander as I peer out the study window and look at the trees outside. The study faces the front of the house and has a view of the tree grove that I meandered into yesterday morning. From where I'm standing next to the globe, I can easily view the woodpecker hole I had seen the nuthatch flitting in and out of the other day. It's almost as if the window had been placed for the purpose of watching the hole. It's a bit serendipitous that the study window at *Nuthatch House* would perfectly align with a tree cavity so tempting to the nuthatch species.

I come closer to the window and push back the drapes that cover the crown molding. On the right side of the window, embedded at the top of the molding, I see someone has placed a large silver nuthatch. They've positioned it so that it appears to be perching on the window, overlooking the study. I peer over at the left one and frown. Unlike the right side, the top left of the molding is bare. There's a nuthatch shaped hole in the wall where the missing nuthatch should be. Someone has taken it.

The solid silver nuthatches are undoubtably what Madge had intended for me to see. I've never heard of anything like them before, but why would one of the pair be missing? And had Madge known one of them was gone when she started writing me that letter?

I put the drapes back where I found them and remember that Charlie needs his glasses back. Out in the kitchen, Charlie is still reading his magazine.

"Here are your glasses," I say. "I hope you don't mind, but I borrowed them for a second so that I could look at something."

Charlie wipes them off on his shirt before placing them on his face. "Something interesting, I hope?"

"Actually, yes. I found the two solid silver nuthatches in the study, or, I should say, I found one solid silver nuthatch in the study. The story about Ralph making them for Hester on their wedding day will definitely be something I include in my article."

"Those were Madge's favorite. She didn't care for this old house too much, but she really liked the study for some reason and especially those little birds." Charlie flips a page of his magazine before looking up at me. "Did you say you only found one?"

"The other one was gone. It looked like it had been taken out of the wall."

"That's not possible. The birds are part of the house's history. No one would dare touch one of them."

"Maybe someone who needed a solid silver bird would take one?"

"What would someone want with a silver nuthatch?" Charlie grows quiet. "Someone who needs money could pawn it," he finally says.

I nod my head, coming to the same conclusion as Charlie. There's one person in the house that we both know needs money, and that's Lois.

"Say if Lois did take it, would it matter though?" asks Charlie. "It's her house. I imagine she can do what she wants with it."

There are a thousand ideas running through my head right now. The missing silver nuthatch just gives more evidence to the theory that Lois killed Madge. It supports that Lois needed money, but more than that, it also gives her another motive to want Madge gone. If Madge loved those silver birds like Charlie claims, then she and Lois could have had a fight over whether or not they should be sold. Madge might have even angered Lois by reminding her that her name was also on the deed, and she was equal owner to the silver birds.

"You're still suspicious of Lois," says Charlie.

"Is it that obvious?"

Charlie lowers his voice, "I'm a little suspicious myself, but I can't place my finger on why. The intruder theory that Harry put forward earlier makes perfect sense, but my gut, which is always right, keeps telling me there's something that we're all missing."

"I think it's best for us to be careful around her for the time being," I say.

"I couldn't agree with something more," says Charlie as he opens back up his magazine.

CHAPTER TWENTY-FIVE
THE DIARY

I have just finished changing into a pair of thick yellow socks that Mom gave me last Christmas and my favorite pair of jeans when a light tap comes from my door. After Charlie showed me the secret room, and I did some exploring myself, I finally got around to asking Bernice about where I could shower now that the power has returned. She guided me to a spacious, albeit dated, bathroom on the third floor with discolored wooden floors and a free-standing, porcelain sink that was missing a chip out of it.

I answer my door and see Harry standing out in the hall. "Is it a bad time?" he asks while his eyes move to the top of my head.

My cheeks warm, and I grab the towel that's wrapped around my hair and shake out my damp locks. "No, it's fine. I just took a shower."

I haven't seen Harry since he disappeared from the library. Like me, he looks a bit cleaner than earlier, and if I were to guess, I would say he took the opportunity to take a shower since the hot water is now working. His hair is patted down and smooth as if he's just ran a comb through it, and his face looks a bit smoother than it was this morning. I'm assuming he's come to tell me what he has discovered from all the old books that we sorted through. Before he can get to it though, I go ahead and fill him in about the hidden room Charlie took me through that connects the kitchen to the dining room.

"That makes sense. You and I were able to get to the dining room via the hallway right after we heard Madge fall, so the perpetrator would have needed another means of escape other than the hall if they wanted to avoid detection," he says.

"Speaking of people sneaking off to places unseen, did you find what you were looking for in the library? You had disappeared when I came back to check on you."

Harry takes a seat on the edge of my bed. "I think I did." He takes a deep sigh. "When I was reading part of *The Vulture We Know* in Lois's room, there was a detailed section in the manuscript in which the main character, a peasant girl named Penelope, steals a priceless crystal from a chandelier in a French palace she's been tending to as a maid."

I sit next to Harry on my bed. "Okay, what exactly does that have to do with sorting all the books in the library?"

"After you left, I finished sorting the books into chronological order," he pulls a piece of scratch paper from his pant pocket. "Then, I tried to think of all the major scenes and plot twists from each book and jotted down everything in shorthand."

Harry turns to me and grabs my arm. His hand squeezes it gently so that waves of heat climb to my chest. I try my best to ignore the sensation because the look in his eyes tells me his mind is still on his notes.

"I found a pattern, and not a good one," he says. "I remembered Bernice telling us that the first odd thing that happened when they were writing was that a mailman slipped on some ice and got hit by a car when she and Lois were working on their third book, *Ice in the Way of Time*." Harry lightens his grip on my arm before he continues speaking. "Bernice said the next accident was a fire that happened on a movie set that she and Lois were working on. The fourth book Lois and Bernice published was called *A Snow-Covered Street in Twilight Moons*, and it's about a young woman who finds out her lover has taken a wife on the same night he promised to run away with her. To enact revenge on him, she sets his family's home on fire."

Harry stands up from the bed and starts pacing. "Bernice also said Lois and her faced other problems, like food poisoning, when they were working on their seventh book. Their seventh book, *The Alps and the Pinnacles*, happens to be about a young widow who falls ill after eating poisonous mushrooms at a tavern while trying to make her way to her in-laws' castle to share the news that their son has died."

"Lastly," Harry grabs my hands in excitement, "you can't overlook the story that Bernice and Lois told us about the destroyed fox den on their trip to the Appalachians while writing *In the Mountains the Clouds Cry*. In that novel, one of the characters, the main character's father, is given a plot of land in the Appalachian Mountains that he decides to turn into a farm. There's a whole chapter about the father getting rid of a den of foxes who keep killing their chickens, and guess what? The way he gets rid of the den is suspiciously similar to how the fox den was destroyed during Lois, Bernice, and Madge's trip to the mountains."

The corners of my mouth tug slightly southward. I think the lack of sleep everyone is missing from the past few days is starting to get to Harry. "Harry, a lot of storytellers incorporate events from their own lives into their stories. I don't exactly understand what you're getting at. Plus, we already know that Madge was behind all those unfortunate events and the curse wasn't real."

"At first it doesn't seem like anything, but here's where it gets a little peculiar. When I was reading through Lois's new edits in *The Vulture*

We Know manuscript, there were all these references to things that had been happening around us. For example, one of the characters finds a dead vulture lying on their bed. It's been placed there as some kind of bad omen."

I squeeze Harry's hands that are still resting in mine and let them go. He seems a bit discouraged by the gesture. "Lois found the vulture in the wardrobe though. It sounds like she's just including it in her reworked version of the text. I think you might need to get some rest, Harry."

"That's not the main issue with her story though. You see, a few chapters before the character discovers the vulture, she comes back to her room after a long dinner and realizes that someone has rifled through her trunks and stolen her diary. The only clue left behind is a small earring." Harry stares into my eyes. "Sound familiar?"

"Did you tell Lois about the earring I had found the night the wardrobe was ransacked?" I ask, standing up from the bed.

"No," says Harry. "As far as I know, you and I are the only two people who know about that earring. When we were leaving her room, and you told me about how she only had one earring in her jewelry case, that was when my mind started connecting the dots."

"In other words, unless there has been a huge coincidence, Lois knew that someone went through my wardrobe and left an earring in my room in the process."

"Exactly."

My eyes meet Harry's, and I know what he's thinking. "Lois was the one who went through the wardrobe! Why couldn't she just say she needed to grab something from it? It's her wardrobe after all." I find my gaze hovering over the large piece of furniture still haunting the corner of my room. "She must've been looking for something in a hurry and didn't want to get caught. I wonder what it was."

"I think it was a diary," says Harry, "just like in the story."

I sink my teeth deep into my lower lip and lock eyes with Harry. "I think I see where you're going with this but explain it a bit more. I want to be sure that I understand."

Harry smiles at me. He looks sincere and boyish as if he's about to open a large present. "With the exception of the mailman slipping on some ice and their editor getting caught in an avalanche—both acts of nature—all of the cursed events that happened while Lois and Bernice were writing made their way into their novels just like the vulture and the earring made their way into their current manuscript. Lois said Madge was the purveyor of the curse for all those years, but if that was true, who put the vulture in your room? And who ransacked your wardrobe? Both of those things happened after Madge was killed, but they both still ended up in *The Vulture We Know*."

"You think Lois is the one perpetrating the curse?"

Harry gives me a simple nod.

"If you're right about Lois breaking into the wardrobe to steal a diary, I bet that diary might be the key we need that proves she's the one who's been creating mischief all these years," I say. "This theory does put a crack in our original one about Lois killing Madge. Remember, we originally believed that Lois might have killed her sister because she resented Madge for creating the curse. With this new theory though, Lois couldn't have been motivated to kill her sister for that reason."

"I think that's where the diary comes in," says Harry. "Charlie told you that Madge wanted her name on the deed of this house, and I found the evidence that she did somehow manage to get her name on the deed. Charlie thought it had to do with money, and while that might have been partly true, what if Madge also knew that Lois was the one carrying out these deeds the whole time? What if she used that against her sister to control her? It makes sense. I didn't get the impression that Madge was the most charismatic character around. Other than blackmail, why else would Lois let her younger sister tag around everywhere she went for her whole life?"

"The diary is probably proof of Madge's blackmail. Regardless of if the diary belonged to Madge or Lois, it must contain anecdotes that prove Lois was behind the curse the whole time and that Madge knew about it and used that information to her advantage!" I give Harry an impromptu hug in my excitement. "How are we going to find that diary?"

"I think we're going to have to get Lois to tell us where it is," he says.

I step away from our excited embrace. "I think I have an idea."

It's a few hours after noon when Harry and I find Bernice and Lois sitting in the kitchen with Charlie. True to his word, Charlie is still guarding the telephone like an honored sentry. I had forgotten to tell Harry that Charlie had also had his phone taken.

"Can I interest you in some snacks?" Charlie points to a plate of assorted treats that are set on the table.

I make a move for a cookie that looks like it might have some sort of raspberry filling based on the bright pink gel oozing from its center while Harry grabs a similar looking one with purple gel. I sink my teeth into the treat and sit down next to Charlie. Nearby on the table, a large, open pitcher of pink lemonade gives off the tart scent of summer.

"Have Lois and Bernice told you the good news?" I ask Charlie and grab another raspberry cookie.

"We were just talking about it. I'm so excited that they've decided to start writing again. *The Vulture We Know* sounds like it could be their best book yet." Charlie reaches across the table and pours himself a large glass of lemonade before making a cheering motion.

"I probably shouldn't be sharing this, but Lois did let me have a look at the manuscript, and from what I read, it looks amazing," Harry says as he takes a seat next to me. He affectionately strings his arm across the back of my chair, and my face feels a little bit hotter than it did a few seconds ago.

A small smile pulls at Lois's lips. "Well, that's very kind of you to say, Harry. It really is in its infancy though."

"Still, I've been thinking about it since you let me take a glimpse," Harry says before shifting forward in his seat and gripping the back of my chair tightly. "What are your plans with that diary? The one that was stolen in the chapter you showed us? Even now I feel like I have to know."

"Well, between the five of us, I have an idea, but it's a bit silly, so I might revise later. But, as of right now, the diary has been hidden in a library. You see, the thief figures no one would look for a missing book in a library!"

Harry lets out a light laugh I haven't heard before. "That's not silly. That's a great idea. How would anyone even go about trying to find a missing book in a library? It would take forever."

"My thoughts as well," Lois says and picks up a cookie from the plate with orangish gel oozing from its center. "Fortunately, the heroine of our story happens to be quite smart, so I think she'll figure it out."

CHAPTER TWENTY-SIX

A KISS

After everyone at the table finishes their snack, we all retreat to our own corners of the house. Lois and Bernice go back upstairs, Charlie stays anchored to the kitchen to keep his watchful gaze over the landline, and Harry and I head to the library. It's not going to be easy finding the hidden diary in the library, especially without any hints as to its location from Lois, but both Harry and I feel up to the challenge.

In the library, Rockey and Rodeo greet us with excited kisses and cold nose pushes. I can't help but wish they could talk and tell us where Lois hid the diary. It's funny thinking that the two dogs probably know more than anyone else about the things going on in the house.

"Don't you think it's odd that Lois still keeps Rockey and Rodeo locked in the library even after the heat has been turned on in the rest of the house?" I ask.

Harry gives me a half smile and holds the library door wide open. The two mutts excitedly toddle out of the room before Harry closes the door behind him. "They might serve as helpful distractions while we're looking for the diary."

"I hope that wasn't a bad idea," I say.

"Should we just start by going through the shelves?" Harry asks. "The library isn't too unmanageable."

We both concur and start looking for the diary at opposite ends of the room. Harry takes the side closest to the door, and I start with the shelves near the seating area. I skim the various titles in the section I've chosen. There's a lot of books on trains and westward expansion with thick brown spines that seem dreadfully long. This meticulous task will be mind-numbing, and I've only just started my search. A bluish flicker from outside in the yard catches my eye, and I'm immediately pulled to the window seat to gaze at the nuthatch. I've been filing away all my sightings of him deep inside my brain so that I can write down my experience when I finally have time to start my article. Today, he's flitted onto a wide trunk of an oak tree. In typical nuthatch fashion, he hops downward on the trunk towards the ground. He pauses his hopping and digs his beak into a thin crack in the bark until he comes back up with some sort of bug. He crunches on it before disappearing into the tops of the trees.

I look back at the old library bookshelves and run my hand over the wood that has been used to construct the furniture. It's sanded down and stained a dark hue, but there's still natural cracks and dips from the original lumber that run through the shelving. Bernice wasn't lying when she said the shelving was as old as the house. It wouldn't be unthinkable for there to be a nook or cranny somewhere that the woodworker was unable to smooth out upon the shelving's creation. I run my eyes and hands over the wood until I move onto the next row and continue the same motion.

I pause right before the collection of Lois and Bernice's books. A long crack runs down the piece of wood separating the collection of B. Bookerton and L. Wrighter books from a section of children's fairytales and classic fiction. The crack is difficult to see but easy to feel. I move my hand along the crevasse until I'm squatting at the bottom of the bookshelf and see that the crack widens into a deep space. The space is just large enough for someone to use as a hideaway for a secret stash of letters, or maybe a thin journal. I poke my fingers into the fissure and press something too soft to be wood. My fingers prod and wiggle until the spine of a light brown journal, the diary, is poking out from the crack in the bookshelf.

"Rockey and Rodeo! What are you doing?" A loud voice rings from somewhere else in the house.

I run out of the section of the library where I found the diary and call to Harry, "I found it! Let's go before they bring the dogs back to the library."

We tumble out of the library into the hallway. Voices rise from the kitchen, letting us know that people are close.

"How in the world did the two of you get out of the library?" Lois asks.

"You two have been very naughty," says Bernice. Her low voice carries easily through the house. "We know that curtains are not snacks!"

Harry grabs my hand and pulls me behind a nearby door before shutting it. The two of us are crammed together in what I assume to be the broom closet based on the mop that's tickling my feet and the smell of cleaning fluids. My breath comes in loud and out sharp as I try to catch it while Lois and Bernice's voices get louder. I turn towards Harry and breathe into his shirt collar, trying to muffle the sound. Clutching onto his arm, I feel the prickle of goose bumps on his skin. I hope that Bernice and Lois will be too distracted by Rockey and Rodeo to hear any noise coming from the broom closet.

Across from us, the library door opens. "The two of you go back in there now and think about what you've done to those curtains," says Bernice.

There are a few seconds of silence before the door closes, and footsteps can be heard retreating towards the kitchen.

"I found them just eating them. Rockey had practically torn one from the rod and was in the processes of really making a feast," Bernice's voice comes from the kitchen.

"They'll be quite difficult to fix. They were velvet after all. They came with the house," says Lois.

"Well, let's have a look at the damage then," says Charlie who has, for some reason or another, decided to leave his post as phone guard.

Harry and I wait until we can't hear a trace of voices or footsteps. We both let out a collective sigh and start laughing at each other. It's too dark in the closet to see Harry's face, but I know if I could, he'd probably be wearing a smile bigger than I've seen before. Harry and I stop laughing around the same time, and the silence stills around us. He moves his fingers up towards my face and brushes a loose lock of hair away from my cheek. I feel his breath warm on my lips before his own cover mine. He tastes like peppermint and spice, and for just a second, it feels like the broom closet is free falling into some mysterious world that I never want to leave.

Harry pulls away gently and opens the closet door. "We better place ourselves somewhere so that people don't figure out we were the ones that let Rockey and Rodeo out of the library," he says. His face has returned to all business as if our kiss was just an idea that passed through his head and not something that sent us to a new dimension.

He heads towards the kitchen, and I follow after him quickly. Once in the kitchen, Harry takes a seat at the table and gestures for me to pass over the diary that I'm still holding in my left hand. I give it to him, and he slips it under his fleece where it is concealed nicely.

Charlie, Lois, and Bernice enter the room as Harry starts to fiddle with a placemat left out on the table. "Is everything alright?" he asks. "Emma and I heard raised voices, so we thought we'd come check it out."

"It's fine," says Bernice, plopping herself in a seat next to Harry. "Somehow Rockey and Rodeo got out of the library and made a mess in the study."

"We have no idea how they managed to escape," says Lois. "When we returned them, there wasn't anyone around."

"That's strange," says Harry. It's a little unsettling how easily he can act. The thought that our kiss was just an act to get me to hand over the diary crosses my mind, but I push it away.

Bernice shrugs. "Someone probably just didn't close the door all the way. Those two can be very mischievous when they want to be, but they know they're not allowed in the study, so I'm a bit surprised that's the one room in the house that they went for."

"Who hasn't been tempted by the forbidden?" Charlie says as he pulls out a pan and sets it on the stove. "I know it's still early, but I'm going to get dinner started. It'll be ready in a few hours."

"I think I'm going to catch a nap," says Harry. "I didn't get much sleep last night, and a pre-dinner sleep sounds like a good idea."

I follow Harry's lead with a surprisingly real yawn. "That sounds like a tempting idea."

"Well, I'm going to go look around the library and try to figure out how Rockey and Rodeo escaped," says Bernice. "Lois, are you coming?"

"Why not?" Lois gets up from the table and disappears down the hall with Bernice.

Charlie whips around and stares at me and Harry until a firm click coming from the library door announces Lois and Bernice are officially out of earshot. "I hope that those curtains were worth whatever you were doing in the library. I would've ratted the two of you out if I didn't find Lois so suspicious."

Harry's face is stony amid the comment. "I find it interesting that two, large dogs managed to pass nearby this small kitchen and sneak into the study without the person sitting in the kitchen trying to stop them." Harry raises his eyebrows at Charlie.

Charlie shrugs his shoulders passively. "Sometimes it's fun to have something interesting happen around here that doesn't involve murder. I figured we were due for some K9 mischief." Charlie turns around to focus on the stove, but I catch the beginnings of a smile before he's fulling facing away from us.

Harry and I make our way up to my room before we settle into the diary I found in the library. It's a thin brown journal with yellowing pages covered in loopy cursive. Harry opens the first page of the book where the owner's name is written out in thick, black ink: *Madge Tundleridge*.

"Tundleridge must be Lois's maiden name," I say. "I imagine she took my Great Uncle Albert's last name when they married."

"What is your Great Uncle Albert's last name?"

I roll my eyes. "You could also just ask what my last name is if you really want to know."

Harry smiles at me in return.

"Finch, like the bird. I recall your own name is Mr. Starling? We seem to have a bird theme going on here," I say.

Harry gives me a small grin and turns to the first diary entry. The handwriting is so loopy and thick that it's almost impossible to read. I can only make out a few words like *fire, Lois,* and *December*.

"Can you decipher it at all?" I ask. "That's some of the worst hand-writing I've ever seen."

Harry pulls the journal closer to him and reads it aloud for me. *"Today is December 5th, and the dastardliest thing happened. Lois and Bernice were filming a movie, and the whole set caught on fire. Bernice was in tears over it. She's always been so sensitive. I tried to comfort her, but she just turned me away as tends to be her way lately."*

"How can you read that handwriting?" I ask.

Harry shrugs. "I tend to be good at deciphering stuff. I took a class on handwriting in college once."

I cock my head to the side. "You took a class on handwriting?"

Harry clears his throat. "Accountants have to deal with a lot of legal documents, so we have to know about notary and all that stuff. There's a lot more to the job than people realize."

Harry continues on to the next diary entry. *"Today is December 9th, and I'm not sure if I should write this in here, but I think I might go senseless if I don't let it out somehow. I think Lois set the fire that ruined the movie set. I found one of her favorite scarves shoved into the back of her closet half charred and ashen. She claims she wasn't anywhere near the studio when the fire happened, but if that was true, why is her scarf in tatters?"*

Harry flips to a random entry in the middle and reads it aloud. *"March 18th. I haven't picked up this diary in two years, but I think it's time I start documenting what's going on. Lois is creating chaos so that she can get through her writer's block. Whenever she's rattled and can't come up with a new idea, she does something foolish and uses it as inspiration for her writing. She hasn't done anything as drastic as the fire recently, but it feels like it will only be a matter of time before temptation takes her."*

Harry skims through a few more pages in the book before settling on another. *"I'm not sure of the date. I had horrible food poisoning last night, and I can't help but wonder if it's Lois again. I found a book about mushroom hunting in her desk, and we had a fancy truffle pasta at some restaurant. If it is her, she could've killed us. Poor Bernice hasn't been able to leave her bed since supper."*

Harry pages to the end of the diary. *"October 14ᵗʰ. I think this will be my last entry in here. I'm running out of space and will have to start a new diary soon (the fact that I even finished this one is amazing considering how seldom I use it). Lois has done something irredeemable. It was on the set of The Timelessness of the Blue Flower. I caught her fiddling with one of the prop chandeliers. I gave her a good telling off about it, but she stormed off to her trailer. It was shortly after that the antique lamp fell and struck two of the actors. I saw it fall myself. It crushed the tiny woman with such force that she was left twitching underneath its sparkling crystals with only her head emerging from the glittering blanket of rocks. Thankfully the ambulance got there in time to help her away. I followed up with the director a few days after and learned that she'll survive as will the young man, but the woman in particular has sustained heavy scarring on her neck. I sent both the woman and man bundles of flowers. People keep asking why I traipse around the world after my older sister, but the truth is I'm worried that if I'm not around, she'll end up getting someone killed."*

Harry closes the diary and tucks it behind his fleece again. "I don't think we should let this out of our sight."

"I don't think that we should let Lois out of our sight. I know we always suspected her, but this just confirms some of our theories. Whenever Lois is working on a manuscript, she seems to be unhinged. Who knows what else she's capable of doing!"

"Isn't she alone with Bernice in the library right now?" asks Harry.

Chapter Twenty-Seven

An Empty Room

I give myself a bit of vertigo from hurdling down the twisting stairway so quickly, but I manage to keep myself on course for the library without too much issue. Harry and I quickly dodge through the kitchen where Charlie stands chopping up tomatoes. He looks a bit flustered at our movement and stops what he's doing to pursue us into the library. He also doesn't fail to take his knife with him which is probably a smart move considering the circumstances.

Harry and I burst into the library and run towards the sitting area where Lois and Bernice are huddled over old photo albums. The two women look up at us wide-eyed and become startled when Charlie runs into the room carrying a knife dripping with tomato residue.

"Oh no! Has someone been hurt again!" Bernice cries. "That knife! It's dripping with blood!"

Charlie's cheeks color. "I was just slicing some tomatoes. I saw Harry and Emma run in here, so I decided to follow." Charlie wipes the blade on his apron to remove any red juice from the utensil.

"What's going on?" Bernice asks.

I pause and look at Harry. We sprinted down here expecting Bernice to be Lois's next victim, but she looks as alive and well as she did when we last saw her. Her dark hair is pulled back neatly from her face, and her dark freckles speckle her skin elegantly. What exactly is our plan? We still don't have a working phone to call for help, and there's not much we can do if we confront Lois now other than try and restrain her ourselves which doesn't sound very enticing considering we have no idea when the phone line will come back on.

Harry seems to read my thoughts as he glances over at Rockey and Rodeo who are curled up in a ball on the old recliner. "Thank goodness!" He runs a hand through his hair and ruffles it. "We thought we saw the dogs running around outside the library doors, so we ran here as fast as we could. That would've been awful if they'd gotten out again." He gives me a pleading look to go along with the story.

"Close call," I make a swiping motion at my forehead and pat Harry on the back.

"Rockey and Rodeo have been in here with us this whole time." Bernice leans forward in her seat and peers out the window. "Maybe you saw two small bears?"

"Bears!" Lois's eyes grow a little wider.

"That really got my heart racing!" Harry collapses into one of the formal chairs near the coffee table, and I follow suit.

"I better get back to the kitchen. It's not safe to leave the stove unattended," Charlie gives us both a strange look that lets us know that he doesn't think bears were in the yard. "Dinner will be ready in an hour or so. Someone should go and wake Natalie. She's been up in her room all day."

My heart flutters in my chest. Had we really gone the whole day without noticing that Natalie hadn't made an appearance? We had been so consumed with trying to find Lois's diary and pin the curse on her that we hadn't even thought about the idea that she might've been causing harm to an unsuspecting victim like Natalie.

"Harry and I can go check on Natalie," I stand up from the chair and smooth out my shirt even though it's not wrinkled.

"Are you sure?" Bernice asks. "You just got here. I don't mind going to have a look."

"We wouldn't want to disturb you," Harry says.

"Lois and I will stay in the library then and make sure not to let the dogs outside since there might be bears sniffing around," says Bernice. She gets up and checks that the French doors are locked before returning to her place on the sofa.

Harry and I exit the library where he immediately grabs my hands. "The last time I saw Natalie was when the power came back on."

"Let's head up to her room. We might be jumping to conclusions. No one got a good sleep last night, so it's completely possible that she really has been napping this whole time." I squeeze Harry's hand reassuringly. His palms are rough against mine with partially healed calluses.

We make our way past the kitchen while giving Charlie a hurried hello. I'm sure we leave him in a mist of confusion as we retreat back up the spindly staircase that we had been sprinting down just a few minutes ago.

"Do you know where her room is?" I ask.

Harry nods his head, so I let him take the lead. I decide not to ask how he knows which room is hers, and I banish the image of him and Natalie caught in an embrace behind closed doors. Now isn't the time to get jealous over what a man who isn't my boyfriend might've done with another girl.

Harry takes us to the last room on the third-floor hallway. He knocks lightly on the door, but there's no response. He repeats the knocking again with a bit more strength so that it would be near impossible for someone resting in the room not to hear unless they were wearing earplugs. We wait a few seconds with Harry tapping the seconds out with his index finger against the door frame. A minute goes by with no response.

"What do we do?" I whisper.

"Natalie? It's Harry and Emma. Could you open up? We need to talk to you," Harry directs his voice towards the other side of the door.

Silence is the only sound that manages to make its way through to the hall. Harry pushes down on the handle and leans against the door. Surprisingly, it swings open like it has been expecting some visitors. Natalie's room looks untouched, as if no one has been in it for months. The bed is tightly made with squared corners, and there's no extraneous items lying around that would imply habitation like a hairbrush or a lonely sock.

"Are you sure this is her room?" I turn to Harry. "This room looks like it hasn't been used in a while."

"I'm positive," Harry walks in and starts opening dresser drawers and the nightstand cupboard. "The few other guestrooms in the house aren't fit for visitors. One of them is used for storage, and the other one isn't furnished. When I first got here, I made notes on where everyone was staying along with a layout of the house."

I crinkle my brows together. "Why would you do that?"

Harry stops what he's doing, and his eyes avoid mine by studying the floor. "I haven't been completely honest about why I'm here."

CHAPTER TWENTY-EIGHT

ANOTHER CONFESSION

"Another lie?" I cross my arms. Something boils in my chest, and an invisible force squeezes my diaphragm. Earlier when Harry had lied to me, I felt foolish for trusting a man I didn't know well, but now that I know he's been lying again, a deep embarrassment courses through me.

"It wasn't a full lie," he says. "Please don't look at me like that."

"If you haven't been lying to me this whole time, what have you been doing?"

"I've been," he pauses, "avoiding telling the truth."

"I kissed you," I say to him. "I thought, I don't know, I thought we might have had a thing going here, but this whole time you've been—what—avoiding truths? What does that even mean?"

Harry lifts his eyes towards me, and his brows form deep, dark edges over his lids. "That kiss was real. Look, I did have to bend the truth a bit sometimes with you, but I would never kiss someone just to hurt them. I would never kiss you just to hurt you."

"Tell the truth then. Now's your chance—your only chance."

"I'm not a hospital administrator or an accountant for some detective agency. I made all that up." His eyes look into mine, pleading that I keep listening. "I did get into an unplanned accident on the road with Natalie, but I had always been heading to Lois's house. My original plan had been to just leave my car at the top of her drive and ask to stay the night and claim my car broke down. Natalie hitting my car just happened to work out for the best."

"Why were you headed to Lois's house? You didn't even know Lois or Bernice or anyone here until that night!"

Harry takes a deep breath. "I was on my way here for work. I was assigned to gather information about Lois, Madge, and Bernice."

I take a step towards the hallway. I can't believe I've been naive enough to trust a man based on emotion alone. Harry was sent to Lois's house to gather information on her? Was he also sent here to kill Madge? Or something worse? I take another backward step towards the door, wishing that I had asked Charlie to follow me up here so that I wouldn't be alone.

Harry grasps lightly at my hands before letting them go, realizing that physical touch isn't the best idea right now. "I do work for a detective agency, but I'm a detective of sorts. I promise I wasn't sent here for nefarious reasons, nor would I ever hurt Madge. Can you at least give me a chance to explain?"

I don't respond. I've given him multiple attempts to explain. How can he be asking for another? He takes another step towards me, but I take another one back.

Harry's expression morphs into something dismal. "It's a relatively unknown private agency. Essentially, we work with the government when they have bizarre cold cases and need to gather more information. I was assigned the Bookerton and Wrighter Case a few months ago because the case was supposably about a curse, and that kind of odd thing usually ends up in our hands. My grandmother isn't a huge Wrighter and Bookerton fan like I claimed. It was me who spent months researching all of Lois and Bernice's books and reading them and watching the movies. I know I sound ridiculous, but I could show you proof if you like."

He takes a step towards me, and this time I don't move.

"Please," he says "I know you have absolutely no reason to trust me, especially because I haven't been upfront with you, but can't you understand why I couldn't tell you about something like this?

I move over to the tightly made bed in the middle of the room and sit myself on the edge of it. A ripple runs through the middle of the comforter when I sit and ruins the sleek look. "I'm not sure what to say." I push my teeth against my lip. "When I think about it, it does make sense. You were invested in the case pretty quickly, and you did seem to know what you were doing, especially that night when we all caught you out by my car." I trail my fingernail up the seam of the comforter. "What I don't understand though is *if* you really are some type of investigator, why did you want my help with the case? Couldn't you have done it by yourself? And why investigate the case after so many years?"

"The case has been ongoing for years. In fact, your Great Uncle Albert, Lois's husband, once worked for the same agency. He fell in love with Lois after being assigned the case and had to retire because it wasn't in his best interest to stay on. A few different people have handled the case over the years to no fruition, and then, I got assigned it." Harry takes a seat next to me on the bed. "And I don't really have an answer to your first question. Something in my heart just told me that you would be helpful with this case, and so, I decided to trust you. I'm glad I did." Harry gently places a hand over mine and gives it a squeeze.

"Lois and Albert," I say. "Bernice told me that Lois married him after only knowing him for a few months. She even told me that he showed up at *Nuthatch Nest* just like you did—on the night of a bad storm, claiming he had car trouble. I don't know how I didn't see the similarities before."

"I didn't know he used the same cover as me," says Harry. "If I had, I might've gone for a different story."

"And the disposable cameras!"

"How'd you know about those?"

"I found them in your bedroom."

Harry smiles. "I thought someone had been in there. The agency sends us out with those as backup in case we can't take pictures on our phones. I happened to need them in this situation."

"If your detective agency is helping the government, isn't there some way you could've had Lois arrested earlier?"

"Without access to the internet or phones, I have no way for calling for help out here. Not only that, but I didn't come here thinking I would solve the case and learn who was behind the curse. My job is to collect more evidence. I came here thinking maybe I could add a couple clues to the file. Madge's death was a complete curve ball that I hadn't been prepared for. I'm used to more demure situations where I gather facts or do some interviews that don't really end up going anywhere. Solving a recent murder isn't my area of expertise."

"When we were in the kitchen and you were asking about me, was I part of your assignment? Someone you were sent to collect information on?"

"No," says Harry. "I came here to learn more about Bernice, Lois, and Madge. I don't know if you noticed, but I was really thrown off my guard when I saw you sitting in the dining room. I knew Charlie lived here, but I hadn't been expecting another person." Harry takes a pause. "I'm not upset that there was an extra person though."

Harry moves his hand up my arm and gives it a soft stroke. "I'm sorry I had to lie to you. I never knew I was going to end up liking you, and I wouldn't want you to think I lie to the women I like."

I lean into Harry's arms, and I'm engulfed in a tight hug. Harry smells like sweet soap and something else I can't quite name, but it reminds me of home. I untangle myself from his embrace and hold his wrists in my hands.

"What are we going to do about Natalie? Do you know more about her as well?"

Harry shakes his head. "Natalie truly is just some person who bumped into me with her car and got stuck here on an unfortunate night. Based on the condition of her room, I would say if she hasn't left on her own accord, then whoever made her leave, cleaned her room up pretty well."

There's a loud knock on the door, and Harry and I both turn towards it.

"Dinner is ready!" It's Charlie's voice. He probably doesn't know that Harry and I are in Natalie's room, and she's completely disappeared.

Harry and I stay quiet until we hear retreating footsteps.

"Let's go downstairs to dinner before we start to look suspicious ourselves," I say.

Harry concedes and we make our way to the kitchen which has been filled with the smells of cilantro and red pepper. Someone has set the table with simple yellow tablemats and white plates. The open pitcher from earlier in the day that was filled with lemonade has been replaced with a closed pitcher of some kind of iced tea. I note the table has six table settings, so whoever set it has no idea that Natalie is gone.

Bernice and Lois are already settled at the table and sipping out of clear glasses while staring at the plates of food Charlie has put out. He's made some sort of chicken dish dressed with savory peppers and plump yellow tomatoes along with some vegetables and scalloped potatoes. From where I stand, the light gleams off of the yellowy butter that soaks the potato dish.

"I'll never regret the day I decided to let one of my rooms out to someone with such exquisite cooking skills," Lois says while patting at her white hair.

Charlie smiles politely and takes a seat at the table. Harry and I join him so that we're sitting across from one another.

"Is Natalie coming?" asks Bernice.

"I knocked on her door, and no one answered," says Charlie.

"We also went to check on her and didn't hear anything," says Harry as he spoons some chicken onto his plate along with a helping of potatoes.

"She was up all night. I can bring her a plate after dinner," says Lois.

Maybe it wouldn't be a bad idea to send Lois upstairs with a plate of food and see if she pretends to give it to Natalie. It might be one way to figure out if she's behind Natalie's disappearance.

Lois wipes at her mouth with one of the white serviettes while clearing her throat "I know we've all been avoiding the issue, but Charlie tells us that the phone line still isn't up. I think it's time that we start thinking about going for help on foot now that the wind outside has finally calmed down. Not only that, but now that we know the intruder is the one who hurt Madge and not one of us, there shouldn't be any reason why someone can't venture out. I say we wait one more hour for the phone to come up, and if it doesn't, someone goes for help."

Lois speaks confidently of the idea that an outsider is the one who hurt Madge, but I know better than to trust her. While I do agree that it is probably safe for one of us to go for help, there's no way I'm going to let Lois out of my sight and nominate her to leave the premises. I poke my fork into the scalloped potatoes and let the salt envelop my taste buds when they touch my tongue.

CHAPTER TWENTY-NINE

PHOTOGRAPHS AND MEMORIES

A fter we've cleaned up the kitchen, Lois leaves with a plate of re-heated food to bring to Natalie. Harry and I traipse after Bernice to the library while Charlie decides to give the landline one last go before joining us. When we get to the library, Bernice settles onto the couch and picks up the photo album she and Lois had been preoccupied with before dinner. Her hand runs down the length of the spine before she fiddles with one of the pages.

"Lois got these old albums out because when we first started writing *The Vulture We Know*, we were planning on setting it in an old mining town, and we had visited one right before *The Timelessness of the Blue Flower*, so we thought we would dig through these old pictures to see if we could find any from our trip."

Bernice pulls out a picture and hands it to me. "We took that one the day we got onto the set for *The Timelessness of the Blue Flower*."

The picture is a bit grainy, but the smiles on Bernice and Lois's faces are clear. The two of them are sitting in director chairs and wearing matching dark sunglasses. They must've been filming outside the day the picture was taken. I pass the photograph to Harry, and he takes it in his hands to inspect it himself.

Bernice extracts another photo from the album and smiles. "This one was taken on the ballroom set. It was gorgeous. The chandelier isn't hung up yet, so this must've been just an early rehearsal with some of the actors. I'll never forget that room. Before the chandelier dropped, it had been the most enchanting space I had ever seen."

Bernice hands me the photo. "It's hard to tell from the picture, but the walls were painted this peachy cream color, and all the molding had been done in a faux gold. I also have a distinct memory of it always smelling like fresh baked bread. It was truly just lovely." She then points to a young man off center and cut off from the frame. "I can't remember his name but that was one of the supporting actors. I think he won an award for the movie."

I study the picture Bernice has just handed me. The room does indeed look enchanted as she suggests. Even without the chandelier, it's easy to observe the grandeur of the space, and the delicate choices of the set designer. It does look like a palace ballroom that's just waiting for a glamourous ball to start and men and women to waltz to the sounds of violins and pianos. In the center of the picture, Bernice is talking to Lois, their heads bent close together in conspiration. There is a flurry of people in the background of the photograph that must be actors and others working on the set such as makeup and hair teams. I study a few of them until my eyes fall upon a petite woman standing a few feet away from Bernice and Lois. Her blonde hair is pulled back into a French twist, and she's holding a script, but her more detailed features have been blurred from the camera's flash. Something feels eerily familiar about her.

"Bernice," I show her the photograph, "who is that woman?"

Bernice squints at the photo. "I'm not sure. Maybe a background actor? You know, it's been quite some time since Lois and I were on that set."

"Do you have any other pictures like this one?" I ask.

"Of course," Bernice passes me the photo album, and there's three other pictures from the ballroom set.

One is a photograph of Madge and a young man with gelled blond hair wearing a tuxedo, and the other one is of Bernice and Lois doing a funny pose next to a sound man and his fluffy prop. Neither photo has the mysterious blonde woman. The third picture is different though. It's taken from an angle so that the photographer must have been standing on the side of the set instead of directly in front of it. A man and the blonde woman stand over a large white X taped onto the floor. The man's hair is dark and slicked back in a similar style to the blond man from the other photo. The woman's hair has been placed in a delicate updo that curls around the edge of her face. The two actors are dressed in period costume and appear to be rehearsing a scene. The woman's back is to the camera while the man's face is a clear shot. Although they aren't the main focus of the scene, another couple in the foreground dressed in brighter colors, they still look phenomenal.

I let out a gasp and drop the album onto the floor. It falls silently before making a small plop on the carpet. Both Rodeo and Rockey perk their ears up when they hear the sound.

"What's wrong?" asks Bernice.

Harry bends down and retrieves the album. He studies it for a moment before his eyes grow wide—the dam of information bursting behind them.

"What?" Bernice asks again. "What's all the fuss?"

Harry points to the man with the dark, slicked back hair in the photograph so that Bernice can see it better. "Doesn't that look like the man from the car?"

Bernice furrows her brows before getting close enough to the photograph to give it a kiss. "It does look like him. It's probably just an odd coincidence."

Harry flips another page in the album and a loose leaf of paper flutters to the floor. I bend down and pick it up. It's an old call sheet with the names of various actors and their scheduled film times. One name catches my eye.

"What's wrong?" asks Harry.

"One of the names on the call sheet is Natalie Zimmer. She's one of two actors listed under a scene titled "Chandelier Montage Clips." The other name is Marvin Zimmer."

A moment passes before Harry understands what I'm implying. "You think Natalie, the Natalie who has been staying in this house for the past few days, is the same Natalie Zimmer in the movie?" Harry asks. "And Marvin, the other actor, you think he's the same dead man we found in your car?"

"It can't be though," says Bernice.

"Why not?" I ask.

"Well, this is awful to say, but I'm afraid that the white X that the two actors are standing on in that one photograph marks the spot right below the chandelier. If that is Natalie standing on the X in that picture, that would make her the young background actress who was struck by the falling chandelier, and she died."

Harry puts a light hand on her shoulder. "Are you absolutely sure that she died?"

Bernice presses a hand against her freckled cheek as she grows ruddy. "Well, no. You see, at the time, people were so careful about what they said around us after the accident. Everyone was walking on eggshells." A line deepens between Bernice's eyes. "If I wanted to learn anything about the accident, I was forced to eavesdrop on conversations and listen through closed doors. I assumed the young woman died based on information I had pieced together." Bernice pauses. "I suppose I could've been wrong."

I grab hold of Harry's arm. "Madge's diary!"

"Madge's diary?" asks Bernice.

I flick my eyes from hers to Harry's, willing for him to remember what I am remembering. "Madge talked to the director after the accident on set to see if the actors would be okay. She wrote in her diary that they both survived!"

"That's right!" Harry is now clutching my arm. "She said she sent them flowers!"

I think back to Natalie sitting in the corner of the room by the heated fire wearing her scarf and gloves. Madge had written in her diary that the chandelier would've left extensive scars on the victim's neck. Was it possible that Natalie hadn't just been wearing the scarf and gloves to keep warm, but maybe, she had worn them to hide her scars too? Even when we had all been playing cards in the library, I had studied Natalie's face up close and determined that she was older than I realized. If she is closer to forty than thirty, she easily could've been the actress who had been the victim of the cursed chandelier. If the woman in the photograph is Natalie, it seems like too much of a coincidence for her to have just shown up to Lois's house on the night of a murder.

Bernice's eyes stare into the fire before they turn dark. "Are you two saying that Madge followed up on the chandelier incident, and after finding out that both of the victims survived, that she sent them flow-ers? What a sick woman."

I exchange a glance with Harry before I remember that Bernice doesn't know that Lois is the true culprit behind the curse and not Madge. Before I can start to explain Madge's pure intentions, someone bursts into the library, and the familiar smell of dinner greets my nose. Lois appears in the sitting area holding an untouched plate of food.

"Natalie isn't in her room," she says.

I'm staring at the dinner plate in Lois's hand when I speak. "We need to find her." I watch a delicate wave of steam loop off of the potatoes on the dinner plate. "We need to find her now."

"Do you think she's in danger?" Lois places the plate onto the coffee table while fretting lines pull at her mouth.

"No," I say. "I think she murdered Madge."

Chapter Thirty

THE SEARCH

The crackle of the fire behind me sounds more like the roar of waves smashing into a jetty. Bernice has picked up the photo album and is clutching it to her chest like a well-loved stuffed animal. Lois has taken a seat on the couch and let her eyes go vacant as she processes my revelation.

"You think Natalie murdered Madge?" Lois's soul returns to her green eyes.

"Yes," I say. "I think Natalie was the young actress who was hurt in the chandelier incident all those years ago, and I think she came back here to settle the score."

Bernice looks down at the photo album in her hand and studies some of the pictures. "I think you're right. When I first saw Natalie, I remember thinking that she looked familiar, but my mind never went to the young actress who was injured because I thought that she had died, but now that I put it all together, it makes so much sense. Of course, she would come here after all those years. She must've figured out somehow that Madge was behind the chandelier coming loose and killed her for it."

Harry gives me a look that lets me know that it's time to finally reveal what the two of us have kept to ourselves for a while. "Except she didn't mean to kill Madge," I say. "She meant to kill Lois."

"Me?" Lois shoots up off the couch and holds a hand over her heart. "Why would she want to kill me?"

"Because you were the one who fiddled with the chandelier. You were the one that caused the accident, all the accidents. You were the one behind the curse the whole time. She must've got you and Madge confused just as I did on the first night, and when she killed Madge, she must've thought it was you."

Lois's green eyes well with glassy tears that makes them look like smooth marbles in the fire light. "How did you figure out that I was behind the curse?"

"We found Madge's diary," I say.

"But..." Lois trails off. "I thought I hid it so well."

"What is going on?" asks Bernice.

"Bernice, the night that you found the wardrobe broken into and ransacked, that was Lois's doing. She wasn't after the manuscript. She was looking for Madge's diary so that she could hide it. She didn't want anyone reading what Madge had documented. Specifically, Lois didn't want you to find out that all those awful incidences that kept occurring whenever you were working on a book were all her doing," I say.

"It's the honest truth," Lois looks at Bernice and the glassy water that's been held back in her eyes for so long finally spills over and paints her face. "I would have these horrible bouts where I couldn't write. I then realized if I did something crazy, then ideas would come to me. It was like a forbidden stream that I had awakened. I never meant to hurt anyone though. The fire I set, and the food poisoning I caused, I had never meant for them to get so out of hand, and even then, I didn't stop doing things after those events since no one got seriously hurt. The chandelier had been an accident too. I had stolen a small crystal from it. I expected the insurance company would go into a tizzy over it, but instead, I learned that the crystal I had taken proved to be rather important to the integrity of the lamp. You see, it was an antique, and when I yanked out the stone, I must've done something to the cables as well. I was horrified when it dropped on those actors." Lois has streams of crystal tears running down her cheeks. "And now, poor Madge has paid the price for my deeds."

Bernice folds her arms across her body. "You were behind everything? Even the recent things like the toy vulture?"

Lois nods her head in shame. "I would do little things to spur my imagination. I knew it wasn't right." Lois's body folds in on itself, and she looks as small and as crumpled as a discarded handkerchief as she sits upon the library couch. "When the police get here, I'll tell them everything that I've done. It's the right thing to do after what Madge has suffered on my behalf."

"What I don't understand," says Bernice, "is how Natalie figured out Lois was behind this curse before any of us did."

"That's probably a question best left to the authorities," says Harry.

"What about all that talk about an intruder though?" asks Bernice. "How does that fit into the equation if Natalie murdered Madge?"

"I think Natalie may have had help," says Harry. "It's possible that she didn't actually kill Madge herself, but rather, had someone kill Madge for her. The dead man we found in Emma's car could've very easily been her accomplice, especially when we consider that he looks very similar to the actor in the photograph."

Bernice stares through the sinking seconds of time. "If you had told me an hour ago that Natalie was the young actress victimized by the chandelier, I wouldn't have believed you, but now, it feels like the most unusual seems to be true."

Harry peers back at the photograph of the two actors. "That man has the same scar as the man in the car!"

I glance at the picture myself, and sure enough, the man in the photograph has the same white slash across his forehead as the dead man. "He and Natalie must've been working together to try and hurt Lois! Then, Natalie turned on him for some reason, killing him in my car!"

Bernice takes all this in and nods. "What will the two of you do then?"

"What do you mean?" I ask.

Bernice takes a seat on the couch and puts her arm around the despondent Lois who sits with her head curved towards the floor. "Obviously, I can't leave Lois alone, and Charlie needs to keep trying the phone line so that someone can call the police. That leaves the two of you to track down Natalie before she gets away with murder."

Harry and I exchange a look. We both know that Bernice is right.

The second time that Harry and I enter Natalie's room, we burst through the door, a tempest making landfall. The room looks the same as it did earlier, but this time we don't hesitate to thoroughly search it for clues of Natalie's disappearance. While Harry makes his way over to her nightstand, I drag open the drawers of the dresser, hoping she might have left something behind that would hint at where she has gone. The drawers are as empty as the air, so I move onto the wardrobe in the corner. Unlike the one in my room, this one is newer with dark wood stain and silver handles. Just like the drawers, the wardrobe is empty.

"I haven't found anything," I say to Harry as he picks up the mattress and peaks under it.

Harry stands up and crosses his arms, having found the room just as empty as I have. "What I don't understand," Harry says, "is why did Natalie leave?"

"She probably figured she'd be caught," I say.

"But there was no reason for her to think that we were on to her. In fact, it wasn't until a few moments ago that we realized it was her this whole time."

"Maybe she thought she should get out before it was too late?"

"Possibly," Harry raises his brows and looks at me. "But why leave before you've finished what you've come to do?"

I pause at Harry's words. Why would Natalie leave? If it had been her goal to hurt Lois, she had been far from reaching it. In fact, Lois was sitting perfectly fine in the library downstairs.

"You think she's still around here?"

Harry nods his head. "What if she's waiting for the right time to strike? She could've packed up her stuff and put it somewhere that makes it easy for her to make a quick escape."

I glance out the window of Natalie's room. It overlooks the woods, just as mine does. The trees sway passively in the breeze and the leaves on the ground stir into gentle waltzes. Lois's house is so sheltered from sight, it would be easy for Natalie to hide in the woods and come out when convenient. The task of tracking her down or her belongings feels inconceivable until an idea hits me.

"If her goal is to hurt Lois, she still has to be relatively close by. If she roams too far, she won't be able to keep an eye on Lois, so she won't know when to strike next. My guess is that she's still around, and she's waiting for nightfall to confront Lois, hoping that Lois will be alone."

"And if you think about it," I continue, "it makes sense that Natalie hasn't attacked Lois yet. The first night she was probably in shock from having killed the wrong sister, and the second night everyone slept in the library together, so there's no way she could've killed Lois then. All the times in between, everyone was too on guard for her to try anything."

Harry glances down at the silver watch wrapped around his wrist. The light lavender face catches my eye. "It's already evening now, so it won't be long until it's dark. Let's tell everyone what we know and figure out a plan. The five of us against her is our best bet to putting an end to all of this.

"Let's go." Harry grabs my hand and leads me to the door. Right before he opens it though, he turns around. It feels like a flash of lightning has brushed against me as he gives me a quick peck on the lips. "Just a reminder that I like you even when things get a little crazy." He smiles at me, and I smile back.

Lois, Bernice, and Charlie are all sitting at the kitchen table while Harry and I explain the situation. Charlie is the most shocked, having been absent from the library when the original revelations about Natalie were discovered. He keeps fiddling with a button on his shirt, loosening it with each pull.

"She won't go for me if she doesn't think I'm alone though," says Lois. "That's why she didn't go after me all the other times she was here. I was always with someone or someone was always with her. We need to create a moment where we can be one-on-one."

"This sounds rather dangerous," says Bernice. "Are we sure it's the right move to take a risk like this?"

"It's the move we have to make," Lois says. "We've waited long enough for the phones to come back, and they haven't. If we don't do anything, she's bound to hurt one of us one way or the other."

"Yes, but putting yourself in that situation seems a bit foolhardy," says Bernice.

"It's the least I can do for Madge. She died for me after all." Lois's shoulders slump, making her appear small and frail.

"What will we do once we catch her?" asks Charlie.

Charlie brings up the one question that I still have lingering in my head. If we do catch Natalie, what are we to do? Keep her restrained until the phone line hopefully comes back up? Based on the damage from the windstorm, that could be days away, and we can't keep her restrained for too long. Demand she gives us our cell phones back since she most likely stole them? It would be unlikely that she would cooperate, and even if she did, there's still the distinct possibility that the phones won't have reception because of the storm. It feels like the sun has skipped through the sky, and we're all back at day one once again.

"Of course!" I say, jumping a little and disturbing the rest of those present. "We won't have to restrain her long because the police will be on their way!"

"They will?" Charlie asks.

"Remember, at dinner, Lois suggested that someone go for help on foot? Who better to do it than you, Charlie?"

"Me?" he says.

"Now that we know Natalie is only interested in exacting revenge on Lois, there's no reason we can't split up, and I think that's exactly what we'll have to do." I gesture with my hands as my heart ticks in my ears. "Charlie, you've lived here long enough that you know where the local police station is, right?"

Charlie nods his head. "I think I could navigate it on foot although it might take me a bit." Charlie's eyes waver to the growing darkness outside. "I'll definitely have to take a flashlight with me, and I'll take some pepper spray just in case Natalie decides to go for me."

"Great. Bernice," I turn to look at Bernice whose dark eyes have growing gray puffs under them, "you can take over Charlie's position at the phone. We can't completely rule out the phone line coming back on, so we'll need someone checking it once in a while."

"I'll do anything I can to help catch that woman," Bernice sits up a little straighter in her seat. "If I didn't think Charlie would get to the police station quicker than myself, I would be sprinting there right now."

"That leaves us with one thing left to plan," says Lois. "How are we luring Natalie back here?"

Harry and I take a seat at the table, and the five of us braid together a complex string of ideas in the fast-fading and fiery light of the sunset.

CHAPTER THIRTY-ONE

THE MURDERER

It's not long before Charlie sets out to get help, and everyone takes their places according to plan. Bernice sits in a corner of the kitchen so that she can't be attacked from behind like Charlie was on the first night. From where she sits, she can see both the hallway leading to the dining room and the hallway leading to the library. She's also near enough to the phone to check it every once in a while. Lois makes her way to the library. We figure that the intruder came through the French doors in the library on the first night, so if Natalie is hiding outside, she most likely will try to break in the same way that she already knows is accessible. The plan is for Lois to make a big show of opening the curtains in the library and turning on the lights so that it's easy to see her lounging amongst her books alone from the perspective of an outsider huddled in the woods. Harry follows Lois at a distance and plans to wait in the dark stacks of the books similar to how Rockey and Rodeo had been hidden between the shelves the first night that Harry and I had discovered the library.

I'm assigned a position in the dining room. It's a stretch, but since it's the scene of the original murder, we figure someone needs to be in the area in case Natalie returns. There's always the possibility that she left some evidence behind and will come to retrieve it. I pace back and forth, my feet making ghostly indents on the plush carpeting covering part of the darkened wood floors. The room feels uncomfortably big now that its empty of any signs of a dinner party. Lois's style is a lot more spartan than I realized. Other than a handful of decorations on the side table, the room is really only filled with the necessary furniture.

A crack echoes through the room, and I snap my head in the direction of the sound only to see that a narrow tree limb has brushed against the window. I'm about to turn away when something in the distance catches my eye. Through the tree line and dense foliage, I see an orangey hue of light flicker. The sun finished setting a bit ago, so the star can't be the source of the light. What exactly would be located at the spot of the glow? Lois's property is huge, so it's difficult to pinpoint what direction I'm facing. I glance back at Lois's side table. It's decorated with a few candles that have purple wax frozen in drips down their sides. I wonder if those same drips dried on the night that Madge died in this very room. I turn back to the orange light when what is happening finally sinks in, and the word "no" escapes my mouth in a whisper so quiet that I'm not sure if I actually speak it aloud.

Something has been set on fire out in the woods. I need to get the others so that we can try and put it out before it grows and reaches the house. But what could it be? If Natalie wanted to burn the house down, she would've set the fire in the house, not in the woods, so there must be something out there that she's trying to hide. My mind only wanders for a second before the puzzle pieces float together in the foggy ocean of my mind. Just like she tried to get rid of the evidence in the dining room, she's now trying to get rid of the bodies in my car! I have to put the fire out before Natalie destroys any more evidence and gets away with more crimes. I make my way towards the door that leads to the hallway but find it stuck as I pull and push against it. Someone has locked me in the dining room!

I ram my body against the old, wooden door, but I'm no match for the behemoth that barely shudders as I force myself against it. There's no other exits in the dining room, so I bang on the door loudly, knowing that Bernice is bound to hear me from the kitchen. I go on pounding for about a minute, but no one comes to my aid. I take a step back from the door and pace back and forth like some distressed animal trapped in a cage, which I sort of am at the moment. I have to get out of this room to stop the fire. Outside the paned window, the orange light in the woods flickers into menacing shapes. I could break the window, but that could prove to be more problematic than helpful if I get hurt.

My eyes trace the dining room walls, willing for a door to open at any moment that will let me escape. *A hidden door!* I sprint over to the old bookcase that Charlie and I discovered contained the passage to the kitchen. In the pantry, Charlie had pulled on a shelf to force the passage open, so there must be a contraption somewhere that allows me to pull this door open too. I run my hands over the faux books, but they're like polished stones. There's white crown molding lining the wall behind the bookcase that comes up to waist height. I run my finger along the top crease of the section that's not covered by the bookshelf, looking for a small gap between the molding and the wall. It's obscured to the eye by wallpaper, but I manage to find a weakened spot and push through the wallpaper, wiggling my fingers far enough under the molding to use it as a door handle. I give it a good yank as Charlie had done in the pantry, and the door bursts open. I don't have a flashlight to guide me, but I remember the butler's pantry being relatively small, so I plunge into the dark anyway.

Immediately I crinkle to the floor and an intense pain shoots up my shin. I've hit something in the middle of the secret room. I grope at the object. It's a suitcase. Natalie has been using the butler's pantry to hide since she disappeared! A curdle of sickness knots itself in my stomach and flips in a small circle. If Natalie was hiding out here this whole time, that means she would've been able to hear us plotting in the kitchen, so she knows exactly what all of us are up to, which means we're all in danger.

I rub my shin and realize I'm bleeding. Something is poking into my leg. I pull at it and find myself holding a dark, circular earring, Natalie's Tahitian pearl. She must've lost it the night she killed Madge. I'm starting to put the puzzle pieces together just a little too late. I give myself a moment to let the pain pass before I stand up and throw my body against the other side of the wall that I know will open up into the pantry. A rush of air greets me when I enter, and I hurry to open the door into the kitchen.

"Bernice!" I yell.

Bernice is sitting on the floor against the wall with a bloody gash across her forehead. At the sound of her own name, she stirs.

"Natalie came through the pantry and attacked me. I tried to ward her off, but she overtook me and hit me over the head with the phone." Bernice points to the broken phone that lies on the floor in several chunks. "I think I was out of it for a little bit, and I'm only just coming to now."

I sit on the floor next to her and check over her wound. Thankfully, it doesn't run very deep. "Bernice, I think Natalie was hiding in a room between the kitchen and pantry while we were all coming up with our plan in the kitchen. She must know exactly what we're up to. I have to go help Lois and Harry, but you can't stay here alone. Do you think you're well enough to get yourself to another room and lock yourself inside until help comes?"

Bernice feebly gets to her feet and gives me a slight nod. "I hope Charlie gets back soon." Bernice pauses to cradle her head for a short moment in her right hand. "Be careful, Emma. Natalie knows what she's up against."

I give Bernice a reassuring squeeze on the shoulder before running down the hallway that leads to the library. My heart pushes against my chest in a steady rhythm like stormy waves thrumming against a seasoned dock. The library door is already open when I get there, so I rush towards the seating area. As I turn the corner where the couch is, I slam right into Harry's back.

Harry stumbles forward before catching himself on the back of the couch. He doesn't say anything to me. It doesn't take long to figure out why. Lois stands with her back facing the French doors, and her eyes locked on mine. The doors have been opened, and I can see Rockey and Rodeo frolicking on the back lawn as a cool air fills the room. Behind Lois stands Natalie, wrapped around her like a snake that's dropped from a tree, ready to squeeze its prey. She holds a silver pocket knife against Lois's trembling throat.

Upon seeing me, Natalie smiles. "I hadn't expected such a large audience for my final act. I must say, the actress in me finds it all rather fitting."

"Natalie," I say in a whisper, "you can't do this. Whatever Lois did to you was an accident and haven't you already hurt her enough by killing Madge?"

Natalie rolls her eyes. "That was rather unfortunate. I was pretty proud of myself until I realized it was the wrong sister. But as my good friend Lois here knows, accidents happen. Just like how that chandelier accidently fell on me and my acting partner, right Lois?"

Lois's face pales as she realizes Natalie's question isn't solely rhetorical. "I'm sorry," she croaks as the metal of the knife presses firmly against the fine skin of her throat. "I never ever intended to hurt anyone. Even to this day, I still don't understand how taking that crystal from the chandelier caused it to fall."

Natalie lets out an awkward hack. "That doesn't really matter, does it? At the end of the day, you're the reason I was almost killed and had my life ruined. It's about time you had the same done to you."

I sense the conversation turning towards a dead end at Lois's unaccepted apology. I have to keep Natalie talking long enough for Charlie and help to arrive. The first question that pops to my mind is the one that tumbles out, and I hope it works in postponing Natalie's main event. "I understand why you killed Madge, you thought she was Lois, but why did you kill that man in my car? You knew him, didn't you? He was in the chandelier accident with you."

Natalie's face contorts into an emotion that I can't quite name, but it looks like something between a cross of sadness and indignation. "That man in the car was supposed to be my accomplice, but he turned out to be anything but." A slight tremor strikes Natalie's hand before she steadies herself. "Marvin was my husband. He also happened to be my acting partner, the same one who was in the accident with me."

"You killed your husband?" I whisper.

Natalie nods while angry lines frame her mouth, and her neck goes taught. I realize it is the first time I've seen her without a scarf. I can make out the fine scars that run along her white skin like little pencil sketches on a blank paper. "He betrayed me. For years, he knew how I wanted, needed, to confront Lois and punish her for what she had done to me, but he always convinced me otherwise, made me believe that it was time to move on like he had. For a while I thought I had moved on, but deep down, I knew it wasn't true. When the anniversary came up of the day my life was shattered into pieces, I knew I needed to take action. I planned a trip out here to give Lois what she deserved. I told my husband that I was going on a girls' trip and made my way here. He must've suspected that I was up to something because he followed me and confronted me, so I had to get rid of him. Those footprints you and Harry found outside of the library were his. He must've snuck into the house looking for me sometime before dinner, hoping to stop me, but I hadn't arrived yet, so he probably went back to the shelter of the woods."

"That still doesn't explain why he was in my car," I say.

"I was in the middle of disposing Madge's body in your car—it was so conveniently parked out front—when he found me. I had a fight with him and agreed that I would let him drive me to the police station and admit to what I had done. Once he was in your car, I took care of him." I stare at the fingers that grasp the red handle of the bulky pocket knife and can't help but think that those same fingers snuffed the life out of the husband that once held them so gently in his own. "I should also mention that it was very nice of you to not lock your car. It made the whole thing rather convenient for me."

I furrow my brows. "I had meant to lock it but got distracted."

Natalie lets out a laugh that sounds like a grackle's call. "Well, that worked out well for me, and I'm very thankful for that. You see, I had the whole thing figured out from the beginning, and your unlocked car was just the cherry on top."

"What do you mean?" I ask.

Natalie's eyes gloss over as if she's gone deep into a trance. "I had worked on a movie set with Lois and Bernice all those years ago, so I knew their real names from the legal documents I still had from filming. I'm one of those people who never throws away old paperwork, and in this case, it truly paid off for me. It didn't take long to find their address, and before I knew it, I found myself researching this old manner house and preparing for a visit so that I could finally take care of some business that should've been taken care of many years ago.

"One thing I learned pretty quickly was that this old house had more secrets than I did. Because the house is listed as a historic site, all I had to do was email the local historical society in town and ask for the blueprints of *Nuthatch Nest* to see the floorplan. I knew I would need to know my way around if I were to carry my plan out right and finally get rid of Lois. One particularly interesting thing about the floor plan that I discovered was that there is a concealed room between the kitchen and the dining room. I stored that information in the back of my mind when I discovered it, and it turned out to be one of the most useful things. You see, that hidden spot allowed me to kill Madge and slip away from the room without anyone knowing. It also gave me a place to hide once I decided to pack my things up when I felt that it was only a matter of time before people started to become suspicious."

"Were you the one who also hurt Charlie?" asks Harry. His voice startles me as I had all but forgot he was in the room too.

"Unfortunately, yes. After Lois showed me how to use the old rotary phone, I pretended to make some calls after they left the room. Once they were out of sight, I hid in the pantry in the hopes of attacking Lois when she came back to the kitchen. Instead, Madge and Charlie entered the room, and I mistook Madge for Lois and, because of my sightline, I miscalculated and hit Charlie. He turned out okay though,

so no harm done." Natalie shrugs her shoulders with an air of laiss-
es-faire.

"And the moving of Madge's body, what was the point of that?"
Harry asks.

"I had been hoping to get away from the house and quickly dispose
of Madge's body before returning to take care of Lois, but as you know,
my husband showed up and made a mess of my plans."

"There's still one thing I don't understand," I say. "How did you
figure out that Lois caused the chandelier to fall? Even Harry and I
didn't come to that conclusion until we found Madge's diary."

"Lois isn't as wise as she thinks. Writers might be able to control the
plot and go unnoticed by all the characters, but that's not how it works
in real life." Natalie smirks. "No one ever pays attention to background
actors on movie sets. My husband and I were free to do what we pleased
during filming as long as we didn't get in the way. I saw Lois messing
around with that chandelier right before we had to shoot my scene. She
was so caught up in her own world, she never realized I was in the room
the whole time, off to the side, minding my own business. Her little
sister found her though. I might've had trouble telling the difference
between the two if Madge hadn't been wearing her signature blue and
Lois her darling green. The two of them had a bit of a tiff. Poor Madge
always tried to help her big sister, and she was the one who paid for it
in the end. I guess she can't help anyone anymore."

Natalie lets out a pleasant sigh. "I didn't realize how nice it would
be to tell someone about all the planning I did these last few months.
Too bad I have to waist my story on you three." She lets out another
dramatic sigh and a visible shiver. "With these doors open, this room
really does get frightfully cold. Of course, I had to open them to get rid
of those mongrel dogs if I was going to kill Lois in peace, but anyway, I

think it's time I finally do what I came here to do. I hope Bernice doesn't mind a little blood on her beautiful antique rug. I do assume that the house will go to her once Lois is out of the picture?" Natalie gives us a wicked smile.

Something flutters just outside the opening of the French doors. It's the nuthatch landing on a large oak tree near the outside of the library. I try to direct my mind back to Lois and Natalie, but something about the way the bird hops down the tree, his face pointed towards the ground without thought or fear, distracts me. It only takes a blink, but the nuthatch lifts into flight and dives straight through the open doors. The small bird zips by Natalie's head! She lets out a surprised yelp, and her pocket knife falls to the ground.

I dive across the room and reach the weapon before she can, snatching the small blade's handle while Lois pulls herself free from the grasp of her captor. Harry takes the opportunity to rush at Natalie and pull her to the ground before securing her hands behind her back. Suddenly, a distant siren can be heard from somewhere on the road.

CHAPTER THIRTY-TWO

THE ENDING

I watch a small red-breasted nuthatch dance in the flurries of snow from my apartment window. After the debacle at Lois's house, I made it my top priority to take some time off of work. While I do miss the antics of Rockey and Rodeo, I don't miss the lack of murders that have happened during my short break.

It turned out that Charlie had been able to get help much sooner than anticipated. While he had been walking to the station, he had been able to flag down an officer and explain the situation. Once the police arrived, they called the fire department to put out my burning car and arrest Natalie. She didn't put up a fight and was taken away peacefully where she confessed to her crimes. Needless to say, I don't think she'll be trying to exact revenge on anyone else anytime soon.

Lois also took the opportunity to come clean about her past, confessing to the various mischief making she had been behind for all those years in an attempt to overcome her writer's block. It turns out a lot of her crimes were too long ago to prosecute, and when the police contacted the victims of the crimes that were still on the table, most chose not to go forward with charges, knowing Lois personally and accepting her apologies. That being said, Lois still ended up with a lengthy sentence of community service and some mandated therapy where she's learned to control her impulses. We still keep in touch, and I'm looking forward to reading her and Bernice's book when it comes out this winter.

The crime that had bothered Lois the most was undoubtable the stealing of the crystal from the chandelier all those years ago, which had led her to believe she had caused the chandelier to fall. After confessing to this crime in particular, Lois learned some surprising news. It turned out the falling of the chandelier had been investigated years ago, and the police had privately determined that no one was at fault. Any tampering Lois had done to the magnificent light had not caused it any harm. Because of its age, some of the antique cables hadn't held up as well as anticipated. The chandelier landing on Natalie had truly been an accident.

It also turned out that the studio had paid both Natalie and her husband a handsome amount of money after the incident and released to both of them the findings of the police investigation. Knowing the results of the official investigation, Natalie still struggled all these years to not blame Lois for the incident. Apparently, she had seen Lois steal the crystal from the chandelier and had determined to blame her despite numerous attempts from her husband to see the truth. Natalie had even made up the story about Hester being murdered at the dining room table to try and convince Charlie, Harry, and me that Lois was connected to the murder and throw suspicion off from herself. The truth was that Lois had bought the dining room table when she moved into *Nuthatch Nest*. It wasn't even an antique. She had paid a local carpenter to custom make it.

Lois was also able to give the crystal back to the owner of the chandelier. She had kept it for years as a symbol of her misguided guilt.

The man who owned the chandelier flew in from France to retrieve it personally as it turned out he was a fan of Lois and Bernice's books. Bernice let me know recently that she's still in contact with the older man whose name she still refuses to tell me. I should mention that he's widowed and lives in a castle with lots of land so that might be the reason why she's so mum on his identity. I'm happy to know that Bernice finally gets to live out her own great love story after all these years of writing them.

After the murder of Madge, Lois decided to put *Nuthatch Nest* up for sale. Since it was the scene of her sister's murder, the old house was a bit too gloomy for Lois's liking. It also turned out that the mortgage, property taxes, and upkeep was too much for Lois. The fifteen thousand dollars that Madge had loaned her were to help with the property taxes. In fact, the hidden conversations that I heard behind the door on the second floor as well as the one while I was in the powder room were both about Lois having borrowed money from her sister. Madge also hadn't forced her name to be added to the deed like Charlie originally thought. It turns out that after Albert's death, Lois felt uncomfortable being the sole owner of *Nuthatch Nest,* so she added her sister's name to the deed herself. While Charlie had heard the sisters discussing money and the deed at separate times, he put the two ideas together mistakenly.

The silver nuthatch that went missing was Lois's doing too, but not for the reasons Charlie and I suspected. Rockey and Rodeo had accidently knocked it down a few hours before my arrival at *Nuthatch Nest.* That was why they were isolated to the library during my visit. They were still in trouble for what they had done in the study.

Charlie and I have also kept in touch despite his constant travels. After everything that happened, he decided to take some work assignments across the world where he's been eating and dining in restaurants that I previously would've thought were confined to the imagination. His most recent postcard was sent to me from a city whose name I can't even try to pronounce where he ate at a five-star restaurant where almost everything was made entirely of ice including the wine glasses and plates.

Not only have I managed to stay in touch with Charlie, Lois, and Bernice, but I've also managed to keep in touch with Harry. He's been busy with his job, especially considering he managed to solve a case that had remained cold for so many years. I haven't seen him in the few weeks since Natalie was arrested, but we talk once in a while on the phone. After all that happened at Lois's house, I finally had time to write and publish my article about *Nuthatch Nest*. Mr. Hawking was so pleased with the article, especially the part about a real-life nuthatch taking down a murderer tete-a-tete, that he put my piece as the cover story. It's definitely the first time that one of my articles has made such a buzz—or a chirp—as my boss likes to say.

So that brings everything up to date. I take a sip of my hot cocoa as the little nuthatch I am watching nudges its beak in the snow. Another one joins him on the ground. They must be a couple.

There's a light knock on my door. I swing my legs off the couch and go see who it is. Harry stands on the threshold. His hair is a little shorter than when I last saw him, and his jaw has a smooth shave, but his smile and eyes are exactly the same.

"I hope this isn't a bad time," he says. I blush as I think about the worn and ripped jeans I'm wearing and oversized sweatshirt.

"It's not. I was just birdwatching. There are a couple nuthatches outside." I stare down at his scuffed shoes. "How'd you know where my apartment was?"

"I'm a detective of sorts. I'm good at finding things out." He smiles at me, and I smile back.

He runs his hand through his hair like he always does when he's a bit nervous. "I was stopping through town on a bit of work, and I thought I could take you out to lunch, if you have time? We could call it a date?"

My mouth forms a smile. "I think I would like that," I say before I lean forward and give him a kiss.

Chapter Thirty-Three

TO MY READERS

THANK YOU SO MUCH FOR READING MY NOVEL, AND I TRULY HOPED THAT YOU ENJOYED EMMA'S FIRST ADVENTURE AS MUCH AS I DID! WHILE I'VE WRITTEN MANUSCRIPTS AND STORIES BEFORE, *MURDER AT NUTHATCH NEST* IS THE FIRST WORK THAT I'VE DECIDED TO GO AHEAD AND PUBLISH. WHEN I FIRST STARTED, I HAD A ROUGH IDEA OF WHAT I WANTED TO WRITE ABOUT, BUT I NEVER THOUGHT THAT EMMA'S JOURNEY WOULD UNRAVEL THE WAY THAT IT DID. THE PRIMARY REASON THAT I LOVE WRITING IS THAT I LOVE READING, AND THE IDEA OF BRINGING JOY TO OTHERS THROUGH THE WRITTEN WORD IS SOMETHING I'VE ALWAYS DREAMED OF DOING. THAT BEING SAID, I HOPE THIS STORY PROVIDED YOU AN ESCAPE FROM THE MUNDANE, THAT IS THE NOVEL'S PRIMARY PURPOSE.

IF YOU DID ENJOY THIS NOVEL AND WANT TO LEARN MORE ABOUT MY OTHER PROJECTS OR KEEP UP WITH NEW EMMA FINCH MYSTERIES, I ENCOURAGE YOU TO VISIT MY WEBSITE: **HTTPS://NICOLETTEHARPFORD.COM/**

ON MY WEBSITE, YOU CAN FIND NOT ONLY UPCOMING NOVELS TO BE RELEASED AND CURRENT WRITING PROJECTS, BUT ALSO A BIRDWATCHING BLOG THAT I KEEP UP. LIKE EMMA, I CONSIDER MYSELF AN AMATEUR BIRDWATCHER AND LOVE SHARING MY OWN EXPERIENCES.

LASTLY, IF YOU ENJOYED THIS NOVEL, I WOULD LIKE TO ENCOURAGE YOU TO GIVE *MURDER AT NUTHATCH NEST* A POSITIVE RATING ON AMAZON. LIKE I'VE MENTIONED,

I WRITE BECAUSE I LOVE TO READ, AND THERE'S NOTHING MORE SATISFYING THAN BEING ABLE TO HEAR DIRECTLY FROM MY READERS!